CW00521612

ANGEL

Sanctuary Book 2

By

Michelle Dups

Michelle Dups
2023
x

DEDICATIONS

This book is dedicated to my wonderful husband.

You are my Kyle.

From the time we met, through all our moves
including countries and all our losses and our gains
you have always put me first, supporting me and
always showing me that no matter what you loved
me.

This one is for you!

LIST OF CHARACTERS

Macgregor Brothers – Leopard Shifters
Dex – Mated to Reggie – Twins Boys – Ben & James
Falcon
Jett
Duke
Zane

Russo Brothers – Hyena Shifters
Anton
Luca

Landry Siblings – Wild Dog Shifters
Joel
Amy – Mated to Rory & Sean Whyte

Moore Sisters – Elephant – Non-Shifters
Renee
Lottie – Mated to Kyle Whyte
Ava – Twin to Marie
Marie – Twin to Ava

Whyte Family – Multi Shifter Family but mainly Gorilla
Annie – Mother – Gorilla Shifter
John – Father to Kyle (Human) - DECEASED
Rory – Twin to Sean - Gorilla Shifter (adopted son of Annie) – Mated to Amy Landry
Sean - Twin to Rory – Gorilla Shifter (adopted son of Annie) – Mated to Amy Landry
Kyle – Mated to Lottie Moore

Reggie's Foster Sisters
Jaq, April, Elle

ANGEL

Sanctuary Book 2

CHAPTER 1

KYLE

I was in the private waiting room at the hospital waiting for Jett to come and update me on Lottie's condition. She'd been taken back there four hours ago.

The hospital had a team of shifter-friendly staff on call. They knew how to handle our metabolisms and how we'd react to certain drugs.

I knew she was in the best place and that Jett wouldn't let anything happen to her, but I couldn't relax until I was sure she was going to wake up.

I tried to get comfortable but wasn't able to sit still for long and ended up pacing from one end of the room to the other.

A couple of nurses came in to check on me a few times. They offered to get food or coffee, but I knew I wouldn't be able to stomach eating or drinking anything.

My gorilla was going nuts in my head, making it hard for me to concentrate, and this wasn't helping my temper any. I thought back to the events that had led to my pacing the hospital corridors.

Our farm had been hit hard by poachers. The MacGregor and Russo brothers had gone out tracking them with the rangers, while I made sure our property was as secure as possible.

Then I left to meet my mother at The Lake, where I'd sent her earlier for help. I needed to have the bullet removed from my left shoulder and the doc, Jett MacGregor, had someone there that would help him.

Along with us were all those that had been injured, either fighting off the poachers, or just by them being stupid fucks. Case in point, the old bull elephant Frank Moore who was causing my head to ache with the amount of complaining he was doing.

When we got there, I got out of the car as quickly as I could because all I wanted to do was punch him in the mouth and shut him up. Walking towards the rondavel, I saw my mother standing there with the most beautiful female that I'd ever seen. She was gorgeous, with hair so dark it looked black. It hung down past her shoulders and she had the biggest green eyes, I felt like I could drown in them. Her eyes lowered the closer I got.

I greeted my mother and assured her we were all ok. My brothers came up behind me, so I left them with her and went to the closest free table with surgical equipment on it.

The old bull elephant was still kicking off, but the female wolf, who I later learned was Dex's mate, had had enough of his noise and shot him full of a sedative to knock him out.

The dark-haired beauty, who I had already named Angel in my head, came over to me and started cleaning around the wound. My gorilla jumped around in my head shouting, 'MINE, MINE, MINE.'

Finally, after what seemed like forever, Jett and Reggie were ready to remove the bullet while my angel held my head still. They'd asked mum to leave but not before giving her approval on my angel so she didn't freak out while they treated me.

I'd watched as my angel's eyes filled with tears that dripped onto my face when they made the incision to remove the bullet. I whispered to her, "Don't cry, baby girl. It's okay."

Just as Jett and Reggie were done stitching me up, the old bull elephant woke up and was shouting out for my angel to bring him a whisky.

She went towards her father with a glass of whisky and offered it to him, only for him to knock it out of her hand.

He then proceeded to back-hand her so hard that she flew across the room, hit the half-wall and slumped down to the floor with blood pooling around her head.

I'd never felt anger like it, clawing at me. I wanted to kill him. I grabbed him by his neck and threw him across the room away from Lottie. Then I told him that if he didn't pack up and leave, my brothers and I would find a way to make him leave permanently.

Once he limped off, I fell to my knees next to my angel. She was still breathing, but was so pale. The pool of blood under her was getting bigger by the minute.

Jett and Reggie worked on her to get her stabilised, so she could be airlifted by the plane that was on call in case of emergencies.

Once the plane arrived, we loaded her, and I got on with Jett. It was the longest forty-five minutes of my life. She didn't wake up once, and I could see how worried Jett was.

When we arrived at the hospital, they whisked her away for surgery.

Finally, during my fifth hour of pacing, another shifter family arrived, so I went out into the hall to avoid making them uncomfortable with the constant rumbling from my gorilla.

The doors ahead of me opened and Jett came through, looking the worse for wear.

He slumped against the wall and ran his hands up and down his face in exhaustion.

I wanted to shake him, but it was clear he was trying to pull himself together. His demeanour worried me, so I was expecting bad news. My gorilla was finally quiet in my head, watching.

Jett turned to look at me, his eyes had tears in them and my heart clenched.

"No," I whispered, my heart fracturing.

Jett looked horrified. He rushed over to me, grabbing me and holding on.

"Shit. I'm sorry, Kyle. Lottie's okay. She's in recovery. I didn't mean to scare you. I'm just exhausted and finally not terrified. I didn't even realise you were there. I thought you were in the waiting room. I was just trying to gather myself before coming in."

I took a huge breath of relief.

He grabbed me by the arms, then hugged me tightly.

"She's going to be okay. Thank fuck she's half shifter or it would have been worse. Frank did her some serious damage when he hit her."

My emotions were all over the place, so all I picked up was that Jett was saying she was okay.

"Jett," a voice came from behind him. A small, birdlike nurse was standing behind Jett, wringing her hands.

Jett turned. "Cassie, has she been moved?"

She nodded. "Yes. I was asked to take you to her room. I've also made arrangements for a bed to be brought in for her mate."

"Thank you, Cassie."

I nodded my thanks at the small nurse who offered us both nervous smiles.

"If you would both like to come with me, I'll take you to her and you can talk to her doctor. Although Jett already knows most of it anyway."

We followed the small nurse through the wards and to the private rooms. Pushing open one of the doors, she stepped aside so we could walk in.

As soon as I saw my angel, my heart seemed to slow and I breathed easier.

I went towards the bed, put my forehead against hers, and just drank her in.

The antiseptic meant she didn't smell right, and there were still smears of blood on her face, but she was breathing, and had good colour. They'd shaved most of her hair off so I could easily see the stitches in her scalp. I knew there was no bandage because we healed faster without them. Running my eyes over the rest of her, I saw a temporary cast on her wrist.

I could hear Jett talking to the other medical staff behind me, but I was content just to sit and watch her. Jett would let me know about anything important. It felt strange trusting someone that I had only just met, but he was a male my gorilla trusted instantly.

Finally, the room was quiet.

I looked up to see Jett looking at Lottie with a sadness on his face that I didn't understand.

"We didn't know how bad it was at their place," he said quietly. "They never said anything. I want you to know we would have stepped in long ago if they had."

In my head I knew this, but I was still a little angry that it had taken this to happen for people to see how Lotties' father had treated her.

I had a feeling my mother knew some of what was going on with the Moores, and that she'd tell us when we were all back together.

But that was for another day.

"Tell me about her recovery."

Jett went over and picked up her medical notes.

"She'll be here at least until the end of the week. Her wrist is broken but that should be fine by then. Her head may take longer. She'll have headaches and some balance issues, but that should all be fine within two to three weeks. She'll need plenty of quiet, and to rest as much as possible so she can heal. Lottie lost a lot of blood, which was the most concerning because we can't have blood transfusions, but her levels seem to be stabilising."

I nodded to show I'd taken this in. Mum would help with Lottie's recovery because there was no way she was going back to that farm while her father was still out there.

Jett looked like he was about ready to fall asleep on his feet.

"Jett, take the bed. I'm not ready to sleep yet but you look like you're done in."

He nodded gratefully and collapsed on the bed under the window. He was asleep as soon as his head hit the pillow.

I pulled a chair as close as possible to Lottie's bed and dropped into it wearily.

Bringing her hand up to my lips, I gently laid a kiss on it.

"I know you don't know me yet, Lottie, but I already know that I love you. I'm going to be standing here protecting you when you can't protect yourself. Nobody is ever going to hurt you like this again, I promise." I rested my forehead on our clasped hands.

As we sat there, I heard someone breathing lightly behind me, but I didn't look round. If it was a nurse or doctor, they could wait.

CHAPTER 2

JULIE

I stood quietly waiting in the doorway, not wanting to interrupt the couple in the room. There was another shifter in there with them and I could tell by his breathing that he was asleep.

All I knew about the patient was that she had been airlifted into the hospital and had landed in critical condition. She had the benefit of having one of the best doctors in the country with her, which probably saved her life.

Her mate had come in with them. Other than his beast constantly rumbling in his chest he hadn't caused any bother, which was greatly appreciated by all the staff. A few had tried to offer coffee or food, but he had shot them all down and continued to pace, eventually moving into the corridor when another family of shifters arrived.

Listening to him talk to her, I wanted to weep. There was so much love and emotion in his voice as he promised to love and protect her. As I listened to his promise, I knew that this was what was missing in my life. I needed a mate who would put me first and love me for who I was, not for what they could get from mating with me.

I quietly made my way back to the nurse's desk and made myself a promise there and then that I wouldn't settle for just any mate, no matter what my family wanted. I wouldn't bow to their pressure this time. Feeling much better now that I had made that decision. When I got home, I was going to tell my parents that I wouldn't mate with the male they'd chosen for me. He was an older male with cubs. His mate had died, and he wanted a mother for their cubs. This was my family's way of making sure that my genes didn't continue. There had to be someone out there that wouldn't care that I was a white tiger.

I also decided that while this couple were in the hospital, I would do everything in my power to make their stay as comfortable as possible, so that all they had to worry about was each other and her recovery.

CHAPTER 3

KYLE

I woke up to soft voices. My head was next to Lottie's hand on the bed and her fingers had somehow ended up tangled in my hair.

Gently moving her hand away, I sat up to listen to Jett and the nurse as they looked over Lottie's notes.

Pulling my hairband off, I ran my fingers roughly through my hair and rolled my shoulders, trying to ease the stiffness left from my wound and the cramp in my muscles which had tightened up thanks to my awkward sleeping position.

While I waited, I studied the nurse who kept glancing at me from the corner of her eye.

Her long hair was tied up into a bun. It was an almost white blonde, laced with streaks of black. She was about five foot eight and had the leanness and grace of some kind of cat shifter. Her slightly slanted eyes were a startling purple blue, framed by dark lashes. Her dark eyebrows were arched, and her skin was so pale it seemed translucent.

When they finished talking, she turned to me with a smile. There was a kindness in her you could feel immediately.

"Hi, my name's Julie. I've been looking after you during the night. I brought you and the Doc some coffee and sandwiches as I'm not sure if either of you have eaten for a while."

Jett was already over by the table pouring his coffee. The smell hit me and I groaned.

Julie laughed softly, bringing a coffee and sandwich over to me and pulling a small table closer.

"There, now you don't have to move away from her."

I blinked my eyes rapidly as my emotions rose. That small thing told me a lot about what type of female she was.

I looked over at Jett who was studying Julie with a certain look in his eye, although I didn't think it was because he was sexually interested in her.

"I haven't seen you here before, Julie. Have you been here long?" he asked her.

She shook her head. "No. I volunteered to come and help out for a couple of weeks as they're short-staffed at the moment, I'm usually at the city hospital."

From the look on her face, I somehow thought she didn't like the city much.

"Do you like it there?" I asked.

"The job is okay, but I hate the city. It's too crowded and there's not enough places to roam."

While I don't shift, I understood what she meant, as both my brothers and my mother needed that same room to roam freely.

I saw a speculative look on Jett's face. By now I had finished my sandwich and was wondering if there was more. As if she'd read my mind, Julie placed a couple more sandwiches on our plates and topped up our coffees from the flask.

"Are you not eating?" I asked.

Jett didn't seem to be inclined to make conversation and seemed to be mulling something over.

Julie shook her head. "I had something at the end of my shift, then went and made the sandwiches and coffee and brought them back."

I must have looked surprised. "Your shift has finished already and you still came back with coffee and sandwiches. Why?"

Jett seemed to be just as interested but was content with me asking the questions. I wondered why, but I didn't know him very well so I was struggling to read him.

She sighed, then looked me straight in the eye. I could see the sincerity on her face.

"Because of you and her, and the way you spoke to her last night after the Doc had gone to sleep. I stayed in the doorway so you didn't see me, but I knew then that I'd do everything I could to make your stay here as easy and comfortable as possible. I knew you wouldn't be leaving her to do anything for yourself. So I thought if that means bringing you meals and washing your clothes so you can change, then I'll do that and you won't have to leave her."

"Why?" I asked again.

"Because what you have is beautiful, and I hope one day that I'll have that for myself rather than a forced mating."

Both Jett and I straightened at that comment.

"Explain?" Jett growled, his leopard rising to the top. I was surprised. Maybe he was interested in her after all.

Julie looked surprised and confused. "I'm a white tiger, and as such not of any value to my family. I'm considered an abomination. The only way I could be mated to a tiger would be by a forced mating. Isn't this done by your species?"

I wasn't sure who was angrier, myself or Jett. The idea that this kind female was being forced to mate with someone she didn't want just to please her family was awful.

"No, this isn't a practice used by other species. Is this what you want? To be mated to a tiger?" questioned Jett.

"Well, no. But what other species would want to have my bloodline tainting theirs?" she asked, confused by Jett's attitude.

From the bed, I heard a voice say quietly, "Any species should be proud to have such an amazing, kind and beautiful female as part of their family."

I turned in a hurry and found the most beautiful green eyes alert and awake, looking right at me. There were tears trembling on her eyelashes.

"Angel! You're awake."

She smiled tremulously at me. "Kyle."

Bending over her, I gently touched my lips to hers and then pressed my forehead to hers, just breathing her in. I felt the tension ease out of my shoulders.

I heard Jett say, "That, Julie, is why you don't settle for a forced mating. If you do then you'll miss something beautiful. Come walk with me. I have a proposition for you that won't include a forced mating. Is the offer of a shower still open?"

"Of course," I heard Julie reply softly as they left, closing the door behind them.

CHAPTER 4

LOTTIE

I'd been drifting in and out of sleep for hours, trying to make sense of where I was and how I got there.

There was a slight movement next to my thigh and I looked down to see a male with long blonde hair, my hand grasped tightly in his and his forehead leaning on our clasped hands that rested on the bed. Moving my hand from under his head, I ran my fingers gently through his hair then left my hand resting softly on his head. A sense of peace filled me and I drifted back to sleep.

The events of the night before slowly started to come back to me as I shook off whatever medication they had pumped into me. I remembered Kyle walking into the rondavel where we were waiting to help the wounded. Everything else seemed to fade out for me as he came toward us. He was massive, making me feel petite even though I was six foot. His long blond hair was in a man bun to keep it out of his face. His shoulders were wide and his thighs muscular. He walked confidently, like he had somewhere to be and nobody was going to get in his way. I watched as he went to his mother and greeted her with so much love. I wondered what that felt like?

As he moved away to allow the other males that had come with him to get inside, he glanced at me and our eyes held for a moment. That moment felt like a lifetime.

I saw Renee, Ava, and Marie giving me sideways looks of confusion. I left them to deal with our father while I made my way over to Kyle. I prepped him for Jett and Reggie so they could remove the bullet lodged in his shoulder.

I remember telling him I needed to cut his shirt off and he winced as if his head hurt. The males who came in with him made some crude joke and were soundly told off by Annie.

It made me laugh that such big males were frightened by a woman so much smaller than them until I realised, these were also her sons.

Jett and Reggie got everyone in place. I was tasked with standing at the top by Kyle's head which I cradled in my hands. The world seemed to disappear into the distance as his eyes held mine. Such a beautiful blue. Now and then I thought I saw a darker colour appear, as if something was trying to peek out.

As if from a far distance, I heard Reggie demand he acknowledge that they would be cutting him open and that he was okay with this. He impatiently replied that he was and that his brothers could hold him down. I didn't feel happy that he was going to be hurting more than he already was, but I knew that he was a half shifter so they'd need to operate as his wound would have already started to heal over.

As they started cutting him back open, my heart felt like it was ripping apart even though he didn't seem to feel any pain.

He said, "Don't cry, baby girl, it's okay."

I hadn't even realised that I was crying until he said that.

Once they'd finished, Jett gave him aftercare and told him he'd be healed in twenty-four hours. He nodded that he'd heard but didn't seem inclined to move away from me.

Unfortunately, that was when my father woke up and started shouting for me. I didn't know why he disliked me so much. He didn't treat my sisters very well but was never physically violent to them like he was with me. For some reason he hated me.

My hands were trembling as I went to deal with him so that my sisters didn't have to. Kyle grabbed my hand and squeezed my fingers gently before sitting up.

I got the whisky my father had demanded and took it over to him. Renee was trying to placate him, but I knew that wouldn't work and would only enrage him more.

I took the whisky to him and he reached out for it. Then he suddenly knocked the glass out of my hand and I could see by the look in his eyes that he was furious.

My last thought as I saw his hand coming towards me was that this was going to hurt, and then my world went black. When I woke up again, it was to the conversation Jett and Kyle were having with a nurse about forced mating.

Their anger filled the room as she told them she didn't think any other species would want to be tainted with her blood.

Listening to her, you could tell she didn't feel worthy, and after a lifetime of feeling the same way, I felt an instant sense of kinship with this female. After a while, I couldn't keep quiet anymore and told her that anybody would be proud to have her as their mate.

Kyle turned hurriedly towards me, and the relief and love on his face made me tear up. By now I had figured out we were mates.

His voice was filled with relief when he said, "Angel."

He bent and touched his lips gently to mine before resting his head on my forehead. His body lost its tension.

I heard Jett and Julie leave the room, and then it was just the two of us.

Lifting my hand to cup his cheek, I asked him, "Are you okay? How's your shoulder? Are you in pain?"

Tucking his face into my neck, he started chuckling softly.

"Only you, Angel, would be worried about me, when it's you lying in a hospital bed after nearly dying."

I was surprised. "Dying? Really? How long have I been here?"

Kyle looked at me, his eyes full of love.

"We brought you in early this morning. They took you straight into surgery because you hit your head so hard. It was touch and go for a little while, Angel. You lost a lot of blood. If Jett and Reggie hadn't been there, you might not have made it."

I was surprised. We shifters were usually pretty hard to take down, but it seemed that my father had hit me harder than I thought.

"Where's my dad now?" I asked Kyle.

He looked at me, his face serious. "I sent him away. Told him I'd better not see him around you again or I'd kill him."

I looked at him in silence, wondering if there was something wrong with me. I felt nothing at the thought of my father no longer being around, nothing but a huge sense of relief.

Kyle tightened his hold on my hands, making me raise my eyes to his. He was looking at me with concern.

"Lottie, are you upset with what I did?" he questioned.

"No, not at all. I was just wondering if there was something wrong with me, because all I feel is relief at not having to deal with him anymore," I answered him.

"There's nothing wrong with you. I'm just relieved you aren't angry at me for making him leave."

I squeezed his hands, then brought one up to my lips and lay a kiss against his palm.

"Not angry, relieved." My eyes were starting to close again, and I blinked fast trying to keep them open.

Kyle lifted a hand to my head and gently ran his fingers through my hair. "Sleep. I'm here."

"But you haven't slept at all either and you've been shot. You need to sleep too."

He lay a kiss on my head. "I'll be fine for another few hours. Your sisters will be here by then, and I'll get some sleep. I'll keep watch over you for now."

I could tell he didn't want to let go of my hand to move to the other side of the room to rest. I knew this because I didn't want to let go of his hand either, but he needed rest.

I shuffled over on the bed and turned onto my uninjured side, patting the bed behind me.

"Get on here with me and sleep, otherwise I'm not going to be able to rest properly."

He sighed, then got up and moved to the other side of the bed where he removed his boots, all the while grumbling about bossy females. Eventually, he sat on the bed and gingerly lay down on his side behind me.

I huffed a sigh at him. Grabbing his hand, I pulled it over me and held it between my breasts. "I'm not going to break, Kyle. You can hold me. In fact, I insist you hold me so that I know you'll get some sleep," I grumbled at him.

I felt his chest shake with silent laughter behind me.

"Lift your head," he said.

I did so, and he slid his other arm under it and pulled me tighter against him.

I sank into him, and the last thing I felt before drifting off, was the touch of his lips on the back of my neck.

CHAPTER 5

KYLE

I was so relieved that she was awake, talking and wasn't angry at me for making her father leave.

She made me laugh when she demanded I get into bed with her to rest because she was worried about me not getting enough sleep.

When I had her in my arms, and I knew she was safe, I felt sleep pulling at me. I knew the hospital staff wouldn't be happy with us sharing a bed, but at that moment I simply didn't care.

I fell into a light sleep holding Lottie tightly, knowing I'd wake if anyone entered the room. Her sisters were driving up from the farm and were expected to arrive sometime in the afternoon.

We must have been asleep a couple of hours when I was woken by hushed voices as the door opened. I lay there with my eyes shut, listening to her sisters as they talked quietly between themselves.

"Oh look, they shaved her hair." This must have been one of the twins because her voice sounded young.

"But not all of it. She's going to hate it when she wakes up. Do you think she's woken up yet?"

There was a sigh of frustration. It sounded like Renee. "I don't know, I've been with you two. As soon as Jett gets here, we can ask him."

"Where is he anyway? He should be here, surely? I mean, the other bed looks slept in and Kyle certainly hasn't been sleeping in it." I thought it was Ava speaking but I couldn't be sure.

"Maybe he's showering somewhere?" the other sister replied.

"Would you two shut up!" Renee whisper-yelled. "You're going to wake them up and they both need sleep."

"I'm not sure I'm happy with the way he seems to have taken over Lottie."

Another sigh from Renee. I opened my eyes and saw her rubbing her temples in frustration.

"He's her mate, Ava. Of course he's going to be overprotective of her, and it's not like we don't know who he is."

Her younger sister muttered under her breath, "She was our sister first."

"Oh my god, will you shut up? She may be our sister, but a mate trumps a sister. Wait until you meet yours," Renee whispered loudly.

"Hmph," Ava muttered. "I'm not sure I want to meet mine if they just take you over like that. What do you think, Marie?"

"Speak for yourself, Ava. I think it's great that she has Kyle for a mate. I hope I'm that lucky one day. I feel sorry for any mate that has to put up with your cranky arse. Have you eaten today? Because you sound hangry."

I was trying my hardest not to laugh at the three of them. I didn't want to move and wake up Lottie, but then she spoke.

"You know, all Kyle and I wanted to do was catch a little sleep after the excitement of last night but, no, you three had to come and act like the Three Stooges and wake us up."

I gave up and started laughing. Sitting up, I watched as they all rushed over to the bed to get to Lottie. The relief on their faces was beautiful to see. You could tell that these sisters were close.

Renee got to her first, her eyes welling with tears. I helped Lottie sit up so that she could hug her sisters.

She put her good arm around Renee and hugged her tight as Renee lost it. The other sisters crowded around the two of them, each of them putting a hand on Lottie. I knew Renee would be feeling a lot of guilt since she was the oldest, but I also knew that Lottie being Lottie, she wouldn't let her wallow in it.

"Hey now," crooned Lottie to her sister. "It's okay, I'm fine."

Renee finally pulled herself together, drying her eyes with her hands, allowing her younger sisters to hug Lottie. She looked at me as if to ask if Lottie was okay.

I nodded at her. "She'll be fine. There's still some healing to be done, but she should be back to normal within a month."

A look of relief flashed across all their faces. After a while, they all found seats and settled down.

I sat back down on the bed and Lottie automatically sank into me. My gorilla knew now that our mate trusted us to make sure she was comfortable and safe, and he sent me a feeling of great pride.

"When are you allowed to come home?" queried Ava.

I felt Lottie's body tense, and I gave her shoulders a small squeeze in support.

"I'm not coming back to the farm, Ava."

That had them all sitting up. "What, why?" Renee asked.

"Renee, you can't be asking me that," replied Lottie.

"We'll make sure Dad doesn't come onto the farm, Lottie. You can come home. I promise you'll be safe," Marie said, looking tearful.

"Marie, you know you can't promise that," Lottie said gently. "My place is with Kyle as his mate. It's not like I'm moving countries. I'm only going to be an hour away by car."

"But what about your horses?" whispered Ava.

I could see Lottie was getting more upset by the minute, and I wasn't going to allow that.

"Okay, I know you don't know me very well, but Lottie doesn't need this added stress right now. Ava, Lottie is my mate and as my mate, she'll come and live with us on the fish farm. I can't leave my mum and brothers to run the farm on their own. That's not the type of male I am."

"Lottie doesn't want to be on your farm when your father can turn up at any time. The property is still in his name, so he has the right to do that."

"I'm not taking Lottie away from you. I realise that it's just been the four of you for your whole lives and that this is a huge change for you all, but you'll always be welcome in our home whenever you want to come over."

"As for Lottie's horses and any belongings she wants to bring with her, my brothers and I will be over to pick them up once she's settled at home with Annie. We have stables at our place. I know that you have a great reputation for the quality of horses you breed and Lottie doesn't have to stop with the training and breeding of horses. She'll just be doing it at our farm instead of yours."

During my speech Jett and Julie entered the room. Jett took the situation in at a glance.

"I agree with everything Kyle said. Lottie doesn't need this extra stress while she's still recovering. When we get back, we'll all come over to help you move Lottie over to Kyle's home. I know that Annie has already started moving stuff around so Lottie will be comfortable. This is the right thing to do. As her doctor, I definitely don't want Lottie on your farm with your father the way he is. It's not ideal for you three to be by yourselves but, from what I understand, he's never touched you three, is that right?"

The three females nodded at him in agreement. Their father hadn't ever touched them in anger, but that wasn't to say he didn't use his cutting tongue on them.

"When it comes to Lottie's care, I'm going to have Julie go home with Kyle and Lottie for a bit to help Lottie should she need it."

I knew that Lottie wouldn't need any extra care between my mum and me, but Jett seemed intent on having Julie come home with us, and after hearing her story, I certainly wasn't against it.

Jett brought Julie over to Lottie. "Lottie, I know you haven't officially been introduced, but this is Julie, she was your nurse last night and will be helping with your recovery over the next couple of weeks. Once you've fully recovered, she'll be coming over to our place to help me in the clinic."

Lottie sent Julie a kind smile, then grasped her hand and pulled her into a hug.

"It's lovely to officially meet you, Julie. Thank you for looking after us last night and feeding Kyle and Jett this morning."

Julie blushed and smiled at Lottie. "It wasn't anything special, just sandwiches and coffee."

"Still," said Lottie. "It was appreciated."

Julie smiled at both of us. "You're welcome. I'm looking forward to helping you in the next couple of weeks. Jett has been telling me all about the different farms and your families. I really can't wait. It sounds so beautiful where you all live. And where I can change and roam anywhere, well, it sounds like absolute heaven. Before coming here I'd never been out of the city."

"I think you'll enjoy it, and we look forward to showing you around and introducing you to all the other families," said Jett, proudly.

Lottie glanced at me with raised eyebrows. I shrugged. I didn't have a clue as to why Jett was so keen on having Julie come with us, other than his trying to protect her from being forced into a mating by her family.

"Oh, here, Kyle. This is for you." Julie held a bag out towards me. "Jett and I got you some clean clothes and toiletries. I also put in a towel if you want to grab a shower next door. The shower in this room is on the repair list as there is a leak, however, it will be done by this evening."

"Thank you," I replied, grabbing the bag from her. Looking at Lottie, I silently asked if she would be okay.

"Go shower. I'll be fine here with the others."

I bent over to give her a quick kiss, conscious of the others in the room with us.

Julie turned to me. "Come on, let me show you where you can grab a shower.

I'll wait outside to make sure no-one tries to get in."

I chuckled. It amused me that she was so protective over Lottie and me. Turning, I saw Lottie grinning broadly at Julie's remark. I winked at her and left the room.

CHAPTER 6

LOTTIE

Watching Julie and Kyle leave the room, I couldn't help being amused at how protective she seemed over our relationship. I had a feeling she and I were going to get on just fine.

I turned to Jett. "Spill, Jett. What's the deal with you and Julie?"

He grinned at me. "Nothing like you're thinking, I'm sure. I don't really know, there's something about her that tells me she's going to be important, I'm just not sure why."

Now my sisters were looking intrigued.

"Have you ever had this feeling before?" Marie asked.

"Only with Reggie. Huh." His voice trailed off as if a light bulb had gone off in his head.

"What? What does *'huh'* mean?" asked Ava, looking lost.

"He thinks she's a potential mate for one of his brothers, is what *'huh'* means," guessed Renee.

"Well, whose mate do you think she is then? You have three brothers not mated. She seems too nice to be Falcon's and too quiet for Duke. Zane is still young and I don't see him settling down yet," I said.

Jett shrugged. "I don't know. It may not be one of my brothers. It could be one of the Russos or Joel. We'll just have to wait and see once she meets everyone."

"About that, why is she coming with us to the Whytes' farm and not straight to your clinic?" I asked him.

Jett's face turned concerned. "I don't want her coming directly to us because everyone knows our family has the clinic on the farm, and it'll be the first place they look for her. I've done some checking and her family are not good people. I want her somewhere safe until I know more about this forced mating she's talking about."

"I've managed to convince her that she doesn't need to go home, but to just let her family know she's accepted another position and she'll contact them when she's settled. Luckily, she was sharing a house so doesn't have any furniture or anything. All that she owns will fit in the back of one car."

He paused and sighed before continuing. "Lottie, she's got three suitcases, that's it. She wasn't allowed to leave home with anything personal. They were trying to make sure she would return. Although after speaking with her, it sounds like there's nothing at home that she wants."

I was growing concerned at what Jett was telling us, and I could see my sisters were feeling the same.

"We can move her around the families if we need to keep her hidden, Jett," said Renee.

"How is she taking all this?" I asked.

"I haven't kept anything from her, if that's what you're asking. As it's only been four hours since I started making enquiries, I've only scratched the surface of her background. She doesn't seem surprised at what I've dug up so far. This forced mating thing has me concerned. I didn't realise families still did that. Her family seems to look down on her for being a white tiger."

"I didn't think that families forced matings anymore either," I said. "Maybe it would be good for her to move around the families for a while until you find out more information. What about bringing it up at the next family meeting?"

"That's a good idea, we'll do that. She's a really good female and I think she'll fit in perfectly with us. It's going to be an interesting few months." He grinned at us.

"Now that Julie's sorted, tell me what I need to expect recovery wise?" I asked him.

He looked at me with serious eyes, "You need to rest, Lottie, and not overdo it. You lost a lot of blood and for a while we weren't sure you'd make it. Your head's going to take a while to heal. You may get headaches and experience some balance issues. I know as shifters we heal quickly, but this wasn't just a bump or even a broken bone. We had to open up your skull to stop the bleeding. I'm sorry to say that I don't recommend you complete your mating with Kyle until you're completely healed."

I gaped at him. "You can't be serious?"

"Oh, I most definitely am. We can still get blood clots and high blood pressure,

Lottie, and I need to make sure that you're completely healed before I clear you for that kind of strenuous activity."

My sisters were sniggering like teenagers. I, on the other hand, felt like crying. What if Kyle didn't want to wait for me to heal and decided that I was too much trouble? Maybe he would find another mate who was better for him.

I closed my eyes to try and stem the tears, but then I felt someone cupping my cheek and lifting my face. "I don't like that look, Angel, nor the tears. What's the matter?"

I'd been so locked in my own head that I hadn't heard Kyle and Julie come back into the room.

Wiping at my eyes, the words just rushed out. "I just think that you'll want to give up on this mating, Kyle. I'm broken and useless. Why would you want to be with someone like me?"

I could hear Renee stifle a sob before saying, "Lottie, don't say that about yourself. That's dad talking."

By now I was crying in earnest and couldn't seem to stop. I felt Kyle pick me up and place me on his lap. His warm arms wrapped themselves around me and held me tight. I tucked my face into his neck and breathed him in, calming down instantly.

From his chest came a constant rumbling of unhappiness and, from me there came an answering humming sound which took us all by surprise. All of us Moores were half shifters, at least we thought we were, as we didn't know anything about our mothers. We had never felt our animals at all and had never shifted.

I moved my face away from Kyle and looked at my sisters in surprise and then back to Kyle who was smiling gently at me.

He cradled my face on its uninjured side. "Lottie, you need to hear me and understand. You are never getting rid of me. I'm a big boy and can handle waiting until we can mate properly. I've waited this long for my mate and there's no way that we'll be messing this up by something worse happening to you. Do you understand me?"

I nodded my head, still feeling the strange humming coming from my chest. Wrapping my arms around him, I hugged him tight and slowly started to relax again. I knew it was my insecurities that had caused me to freak out.

"At least it seems our animals agree anyway," said Kyle. "Angel, I have to say I really fucking hate your dad and there's absolutely no way he's getting anywhere near you again."

He spoke to my sisters again, and the Alpha that I knew he was came out in his voice.

"You're going to have to get over Lottie not coming home, because she's not stepping a foot onto your place until he's either gone from this town or dead. Do I make myself clear?"

My sisters all nodded in understanding.

"Right," I heard Jett say. "Lottie needs to rest, and I have a shopping list here from Dex for the staff at Kyle's place. You girls can come help me get that sorted so that I can take it out on the plane when I leave this afternoon. You can all visit with Lottie again this evening."

"We still need to book into a hotel anyway," replied Renee.

Julie cleared her throat. "You can stay with me if you like. It's only one bedroom but the couch is comfy and there are a couple of blow-up mattresses in the garage. You can have my bed, Renee. I'm happy to sleep on a mattress."

"That would be lovely, Julie, thank you," Renee said. She stood up and indicated to the rest of the girls that it was time to go. They all stood up too.

Kyle gently lay me back down on the bed but didn't let go of my hand.

"Jett, are you going to the Vans' camping place on main street for the tents?" asked Kyle.

Jett jerked his chin. "Yeah, thought it would be easiest to get all the equipment from there."

Kyle nodded in agreement. "We have an account with them. Have them put everything on there and I'll be in tomorrow to pay. I'll give the manager a call now so he can start getting everything ready for you to pick up."

Tapping on the door frame with his hand, Jett lifted his head in acknowledgement. "Okay, that's good." Pointing his finger at me, he said firmly, "Rest up, Lottie, and I'll see you at the end of the week when I come with Julie to take you home."

With a wave and blown kisses, my sisters, Julie and Jett all left, leaving me with a silent room and Kyle looking at me.

"No more feeling unworthy, Lottie. If it takes our entire lifetime, I'll make you see that you're worth everything to me. From now on, you'll only have good things happen to you. I'll make sure of that."

My eyes filled with tears again. Pulling him closer to me, I rested my forehead on his.

"Okay, I'll try my best, but you may have to remind me. I don't know what I did to deserve you, Kyle. I never thought I would say this, but I'm so thankful that the poachers hit your farm last night."

He chuckled with me, kissing my forehead. "Me too, Angel, me too."

Tucking me back into bed, he sat down next to me, rubbing a hand over my forehead. "Sleep. I'm here."

My eyes closed and, once again, I felt the humming in my chest as a deep sense of contentment filled me.

CHAPTER 7

KYLE

Lottie and I spent the rest of the time she was in the hospital getting to know each other. I found her to be as sweet and kind as I'd expected. We also found we had a similar sense of humour and family values. She loves her sisters and would do anything for them, which was just how I felt about my mother and brothers.

She told me about growing up without parents. As far as they were aware, Renee's mother was still alive somewhere, but Lottie's mother and the twins' mother were both dead. Her father had been absent most of the time and that was the way they preferred it. Her grandmother on her father's side had brought them up until she passed away when Lottie was a teenager. They all had fond memories of her. After she had passed away, the girls were sent to a boarding school until they graduated and then brought back to run the farm. All the girls did online courses and qualified in business management and accounting. The twins were busy doing a course in advertising and web design.

I told her about my mother's set up at home, making and selling pickles and jams. I also told her about the fish farm and that I was in charge of running it while my brothers were busy making furniture and doing custom paint jobs, mostly on motorcycles.

I told her that people were willing to pay well for one of Sean's designs. I said I thought it was nuts the amount of money people would pay to have their bikes painted by him, but he made a great living from it, as did Rory with his furniture. They were both fully booked for the next two years and were desperate for help with the administration side as were my mother and me.

I looked at her hopefully, maybe she would be willing to take it over and put us out of our misery?

Lottie laughed at me, her eyes sparkling. "Don't look at me. I'm rubbish at admin. Renee's always on my case because I keep forgetting to file shit."

"Ah well, I guess you can't be completely perfect," I replied, poking her gently in the side.

"Hey." she squirmed away from me, laughing.

It was a beautiful sight. She was doing so much better than she had been at the beginning of the week, not so dizzy or feeling as nauseous. She still tired easily, but according to Julie this was normal after the amount of blood she'd lost. She did a lot of sleeping which was helping with her healing.

She was sitting on the bed, her long bare legs crossed, wearing shorts and a green tank top that made her eyes even greener. The fan above her bed was circling lazily, but not doing much, basically just moving the hot air around the room. We had taken to opening the window during the day, but since there was no mosquito gauze on them, we had to close them at night. I was already planning on making a donation to have gauze added to all the windows in the hospital.

I thought to myself that I must have done something right to be gifted with such a beautiful mate, and she was beautiful, right down to her soul. How she managed to be such a kind and stunning person, despite the way her father had treated her, amazed me.

"What?" she asked, looking at me with her head slightly tilted. The side of her head that hadn't been shaved was still long and we'd plaited it earlier to keep it out the way. She'd decided that she wanted it all shaved off when we got home as her scalp would have healed over enough. My heart was hurt at the thought of all her hair being shaved off, but I knew it would grow back.

Not being able to help myself, I picked her up and moved her to my lap, wrapping my arms around her so I could bury my face in the crook of her neck, inhaling the scent that was all Lottie. Biting down gently on her neck, I felt her shiver and goosebumps appeared on her arms. Kissing her slender column, I hugged her tight against me, feeling her snuggle back and sink into me.

I tilted her head back gently against my shoulder so I could see her eyes.

She looked puzzled. Her hand came up and buried itself in my hair and pulled it out of the hair tie that I had it up in so that it fell around us. As she ran her fingers through my hair, I closed my eyes. "Are you okay?" she whispered in concern.

I gave her another kiss, this time on her mouth, careful not to jar her head. When I was done, I smiled at her.

"I'm perfect. Just thinking of how lucky I am to have ended up with you as a mate."

Her face softened as she looked at me. "Oh, Kyle, I'm the lucky one. Do you know how wonderful I feel to finally have someone that's no one else's, just mine alone? I can't wait to leave here tomorrow and start getting on with the rest of our lives."

As she tucked her head back onto my shoulder, her forehead resting against my neck, my gorilla started rumbling in contentment. As always there was an answering humming from Lottie.

We sat like that until I felt her breathing start to deepen, and I knew she'd fallen asleep. I gently lifted her and laid her down on the bed. I covered her with a sheet and ran my hand gently across her head.

I quietly packed up all our stuff, ready for Jett and Julie to pick us up tomorrow and take us back home. I wasn't looking forward to the four-hour drive. Unfortunately, the pilot we usually used had retired due to bad eyesight. At the next family meeting, we would discuss what could be done about the situation. Both my brothers could pilot planes but didn't want to be tied down to doing it constantly. Hopefully, we'd come up with a solution.

My phone lit up to show my mother was calling, just as she had done every night we'd been here.

"Hey, Mama, all good on the farm?" I said, keeping my voice low.

"Hi, baby, of course it's good. Your brothers and I are managing just fine. We're getting up at 3am tomorrow to load the refrigerated truck for this week's fish deliveries. You'll probably pass it on the way in. Rory's driving it this week."

"Tell him I said, *'thank you'*. I know he's newly mated too, so I appreciate him taking time away to do this."

"They're your brothers. They don't mind, you know that."

"I know, mama, just not used to having them home. I've been so used to it just being you and me that I've forgotten what it's like to have extra support."

From the background, I heard Rory shout, "You had better get used to it, baby bro. We aren't going anywhere."

I chuckled when I heard his mate Amy shush him and tell him to stop interrupting his mother's conversation. My mother was laughing too. I couldn't wait to see them all tomorrow.

"Love you, mama. I'll see you tomorrow. We can't wait to be home."

"Bye, honey. Get some sleep and we'll see you tomorrow. I'd better go and save your brother from Amy," she said, laughing as she hung up.

Switching off the light, I went back to the bed and got in behind Lottie, pulling her tightly into my body. I dropped a kiss on the back of her head and drifted off to sleep. Tomorrow, we'd be sleeping in my custom-made bed which would fit us perfectly.

CHAPTER 8

LOTTIE

I woke to a rooster crowing in the distance. I was warm and safe held in Kyle's arms. We hadn't closed the curtains last night before going to bed, so I saw the sun just rising over the hills, painting the sky a beautiful purple, shot through with hints of gold. The hospital was quiet. It was still early, not yet five in the morning, but I'd woken up with more energy than I had all week.

It was exciting to start my life with Kyle. I'd been speaking to Annie on the phone a lot during this week, listening to her ideas for making changes to the house to better suit us all. I'd protested that she didn't need to go to any trouble, but she just told me to hush, and that she'd been blessed with two daughters in the space of one night and was going to make sure we knew we were valued. This made my eyes fill with tears, but as I was on a call with both her and Amy, I didn't feel too bad about getting emotional.

Amy was mated to both Sean and Rory, Kyle's older brothers. I'd known Amy my entire life, so I knew she'd make a perfect mate for any male, or any two males for that matter. The three of them had moved into the small two-bedroom cottage at the back of the property, on the other side of Annie's vegetable garden. It had needed some work to make it habitable. This had been done quickly this week in preparation for us arriving today, and now they were settled in.

The plan was to build a house for them on the border between the Whytes' farm and the Landry farm, so that Amy could still help her brother Joel with the day-to-day running of their farm without having to travel an hour a day each way. I knew Joel was relieved as he was struggling to work the farm by himself.

Their parents had decided to retire away from the farm and none of their siblings were interested in helping to work the farm.

Once their house was built, Annie planned to move into the cottage so Kyle and I could have the main house. I felt so guilty that they were making so many changes just because of our mating. They all told me not to worry as fixing up the cottage had always been on the plans and that our mating had just pushed the timeline up a little.

Kyle's breathing changed and I knew he was awake, but not only by the change in his breathing. There was also the hardness I felt pushing against my backside. Grinding back against him I heard him groan and felt his hand on my hip, holding me still.

Turning over, I fitted my mouth to his and lost myself in his taste, rocking gently against him. Our kisses slowed down and he pulled his mouth away from mine so he could pull me close. He buried his face into my neck and took a deep breath, holding it before letting it out slowly. I felt so guilty knowing how hard it was for him to hold back from mating. It had been easier at the beginning of the week when I wasn't feeling well, however now as I started feeling better, the mating pull was hard to ignore.

I loved the small kisses he dropped all over my face. Finally, with one last kiss, I opened my eyes to see him smiling down at me. I couldn't help but smile back at the happiness shining out from him.

"Morning, Angel."

"Morning, honey."

He stretched out, his bones cracking after being scrunched up all night in the small bed. Looking down at his body, I saw the evidence of his arousal pushing up against his sleep shorts.

He touched my face.

"Ignore it, Angel."

I snorted with amusement, "I can't. It's right there and I feel so guilty that we can't bond yet. I'm worried for you, because that can't be comfortable. I wish you would let me help you."

"Nope. We need to keep your blood pressure down so no playing for you." He grinned.

I huffed at him, making him laugh. I couldn't believe how well he was handling it. Better than me, that's for sure.

"I could just watch," I replied.

He continued to laugh at me as he got off the bed. "And how is that going to keep your blood pressure down, mmh?" He smirked.

Then came my favourite morning ritual. Kyle reached up to the ceiling stretching his arms and, my eyes travelled down his body, stopping on the bars he had pierced through his nipples, following his happy trail down to that delicious vee that ended just above the band of his shorts.

My mate was a gorgeous specimen of maleness. After a huge yawn, he brought his hands down to rub his stomach, then shook his arms out. Lifting his hands to his hair he undid his bun, letting his hair out and running his fingers through it, before smoothing it and tying his hair back up.

When he was done, he smiled down at me before bending and pressing a light kiss to my lips.

"Are you ready to get up and shower before Jett and Julie get here, or do you want to wait for Julie?"

"I want to shower with you even if we can't do anything," I replied, standing up from the bed and moving to the bathroom. This would be the first time we had showered together. Before now, Julie had been here to help me during the day while Kyle left to do business in town.

It wasn't a huge shower but certainly big enough for the two of us. I knew that while we couldn't complete the bonding, this would go a long way to easing the continuous need.

I switched on the water and turned to take off my clothes, only to find Kyle standing in the doorway watching me with heated eyes. I knew that with my half-shaved head I didn't look my best, but this never seemed to bother him. I still felt a little self-conscious and insecure though. Taking a deep breath, I pulled my tank top off and then pushed my shorts down until I was standing naked in front of him. I waited as he continued to run his eyes over me. Shifting my feet, I started to cover myself as he continued to just watch me.

He gently grabbed my hand when I reached for a towel.

In a guttural voice, he uttered, "Don't! God, you are so gorgeous." Bending, he pressed kisses to the top of my breast then made his way down, pulling my nipple into his mouth while one of his hands covered my other breast. I felt a throb deep in my pussy as he switched breasts.

He pulled away, then blew gently on to my nipples until they puckered tightly. My breathing was coming fast and hard.

He closed his eyes and leaned his forehead on mine.

"I think we need to shower separately, Lottie."

Grabbing his hands, I shook my head and pulled him with me into the shower.

"No, we need this, Kyle. We won't do anything else, but it's three weeks and I need the closeness. I think you do too."

I put my head under the cool water, hoping it would help cool my need. Moving out of the spray, I swapped with him and let him get under the stream of water. This gave me the chance to take in his gorgeous backside. Yep, I was certainly an arse girl, and my male had an arse that I wanted to grip hard while he was in me.

Shaking my head slightly, I thought to myself, *'Get a grip, girl. No sexy times as per the doctor. It's going to be a long three weeks!'*

Grabbing the body wash and a loofah, I moved to him and ran the loofah across his back, massaging him as I made my way across his broad shoulders and down his back towards his arse, then to his muscular legs. Finally, I stood back up and rinsed the soap from him. All this time, he had stood quietly with his hands on the wall and his head bent down. I gently pushed his shoulders to get him to turn around. When he turned, I could see the need in his eyes. Looking down, I saw he was gripping his cock. It was beautiful. Long and thick with pre-cum seeping from the end of it. My mouth watered, wanting a taste, but

I knew he would never let me go there until I was fully recovered. Moving his hand from his cock, I grasped him in my hand still slick with soap and rubbed at the pre-cum that was seeping from his crown.

He shook his head and went to take my hand away from his cock. I gently put my other hand on the side of his face. "Kyle, let me. I promise I'm okay to do this. It hurts me more to see you need me and not being allowed to do anything about it."

By now he was shaking from holding back. Pulling my hand up his cock in a twisting motion, I licked and kissed my way across his chest, tugging on the bars he had through his nipples. This brought a deep groan from him. Moving over to the other one I did the same, all the time working his cock. With my other hand, I pulled down gently on his balls. He lifted my face from his chest and brought his mouth down on mine in a hot, wet, deep kiss, that elicited a moan from me. His chest started rumbling and mine replied in the same humming tone as before.

I mimicked the rhythm of his tongue as I pumped his cock with my hand. Before long I felt him tense and then a hot spurt of cum shot onto my hand. I didn't stop until he started to soften, then gently continued while we kissed.

Opening my eyes, I looked up at him and smiled. With a last gentle kiss on my lips, he wrapped both arms tight around me. Without a word, he grabbed the loofah and soap and gently started washing me.

Once we were clean, we got out and he tenderly dried me off. We still hadn't said anything but it wasn't necessary. Our animals were reaching out to each other in tone, and this brought with it a deep sense of peace.

Kyle gently brushed my hair on the uninjured side of my head and then re-braided it. When he was done, he pressed a soft kiss to my forehead, each cheek, and then my lips.

When he was dry, he reached for our clothes and tenderly dressed me, dropping soft kisses as he covered each part of me. When we were done, he tugged me to him, his eyes soft as they looked into mine.

"Love you, Angel."

Holding his face in my hands, I smiled up at him before pressing a kiss to his lips.

Just then I heard the door open and the sound of Jett and Julie's voices. It was time to get on the road and start a new chapter of my life.

CHAPTER 9

KYLE

Stepping back into the hospital room after Lottie had just blown my mind, I was feeling relaxed and had a happy buzz going. Jett lifted an eyebrow and I couldn't help but roll my eyes at him.

I knew he didn't fully understand the mating pull, because until you found your mate you didn't know how strong that need to bond was. We had to wait at least until Lottie no longer had headaches, I knew that, but I also knew she was struggling as much as me to hold back from bonding fully.

We'd manage though. Once we got to the farm and were kept busier, I knew it would become slightly easier.

"As you're both up and ready, shall we get on the road?" asked Jett.

I nodded. "Yeah, we're ready. What about Lottie's discharge and the hospital bill?"

He held up a bunch of papers. "Discharge is done, and we've got a payment plan set up, so no payment is necessary at the moment."

I grabbed the bags that were sitting packed on the end of the bed, while Julie got Lottie settled in a wheelchair for our walk to the car. All the flowers Lottie had been sent had gone to the geriatric ward so they wouldn't go to waste. After a quick check to see we hadn't left anything, I went over to the doorway where they were all waiting.

Lottie smiled at me, her eyes shining with excitement.

"Ready, Angel?" I asked her.

"So ready, honey," she replied, bouncing in her chair in excitement.

Julie and Jett were both laughing at her.

"What?" she exclaimed. "I've been stuck here for a week. I can't wait to get out. As nice as everyone has been, I need a comfortable bed to sleep in."

"Let's get out of here then," laughed Julie, pushing Lottie toward the doors that led out of the hospital.

Once outside, we went over to the double cab 4x4 parked in the pickup bay in front of the hospital. Putting our luggage in the back, I helped Jett cover it up with a tarpaulin to protect it from the dust of the road.

Julie helped Lottie into the back with pillows and blankets so she could be as comfortable as possible. Walking back round from tying everything down, I saw Jett at Lottie's open window with a bottle of water and a box of painkillers arguing with her about taking them.

"I'm fine, Jett, I don't need them right now. Maybe once we stop for breakfast."

"It's a long journey, Lottie. I don't want you in any pain while we're travelling."

Julie looked at me and rolled her eyes. I had to hide a smile at her sassiness. She was certainly feeling more comfortable around us.

In an exasperated voice, Julie said, "Jett leave her alone. Lottie can take a pain pill when we stop for breakfast. It'll be better for her to take it on a full stomach anyway. She'll probably be ready to crash for a while by then. Now, who's sitting where?"

I smiled at Julie as I opened the front passenger door and helped her into the vehicle. Muttering quietly so Jett couldn't hear, "Thank you, Julie. Those two are like siblings once they get started, they just carry on and on. I thought we'd be here all day."

She sniggered and patted my hand. Jett was getting in on the driver's side muttering about *'stubborn females,'* which just caused the three of us to laugh at him.

Getting in the back, I tried to get as comfortable as possible in the cramped room that we had in the back seats.

Lottie turned to me. "Kyle, sit in the front. I'll be fine in the back and Julie can keep me company," she urged.

"I'll be fine for a little while. Maybe after breakfast," I replied. Not that I had any intention of sitting in the front, that was too far away from her. I would gladly put up with a little discomfort to stay right next to her.

Finally, when I was as comfortable as I was going to get, I pulled Lottie over to me and buckled her in. Then put my arm around her shoulder and rested her head on my chest. When I'd done what I could to make us both as comfortable as we were going to get considering the tight constraints of the vehicle, I realised there was total silence in the car. I looked up to find them all looking at me in amusement.

"What?" I asked, confused.

All three of them started laughing. After a while, Lottie wiped the tears of laughter from her face and patted me on the chest, her shoulders still shaking.

Her voice was full of laughter. "It's the way you just pull me around and put me where you want me without asking."

I was confused. "Do you not want to be sitting next to me?"

"Of course, I do."

"So what's funny about that?"

"Honey, it's the fact that you just move me around like it's nothing."

"Angel, I'm not getting it. Are you happy and comfortable next to me?"

"Yes, I am, but, honey, you have to know I'm not a tiny female nor am I lightweight."

I shrugged, "You're tiny to me and it saves time and arguing. I figure if you didn't want to sit with me like this you would just move and I would adjust until we were both comfortable."

Lottie just shook her head at me with an amused grin. She kissed my chin then snuggled back down. Still confused a little, I dropped a kiss on the top of her head.

Looking up, I saw Jett looking at me through the rear-view mirror.

"Huh, I need to remember that if I ever find a mate." He laughed out loud when I gave him the finger.

Still laughing, he put the car in gear and pulled out of the hospital onto the main road. It was barely six in the morning so there was little traffic and we made it out of town within half an hour.

About two hours after we left town, we hit the dirt road that would take us to the ranches and farms in our area. I knew we would probably stop at the rest stop about ten minutes from the end of the road and I was right when Jett put on our indicator to pull off the road.

This was a popular rest stop with huge trees that provided lots of shade in the heat of the day. It was an old rest stop too. The picnic tables and benches had been here for over sixty years. After being stuck in the car for a couple of hours, we were all ready to get out and stretch our legs. I knew the next few hours would be a lot more uncomfortable as the dirt roads weren't the best. At least it hadn't rained in the last couple of days so we wouldn't have to contend with any flooding.

We passed Rory, Amy and Sean going in the opposite direction about half an hour ago, so I at least knew they'd made it safely so far.

Jett pulled to a stop near one of the picnic tables. We all got out and stretched, shaking out the kinks. I turned to help Lottie out and saw that her face was tight with pain and the sun seemed to be hurting her eyes.

"Here, Kyle, give her these to put on." Julie handed me a pair of sunglasses. "The glare is hurting her eyes and making her headache worse."

"Thanks, Julie." I settled the sunglasses gently on Lottie's face and I could see the relief was immediate.

"Better?" I asked.

"Yeah, much better," Lottie nodded. "Thanks, Julie. Not sure what I'd do without you."

Julie just laughed and made shooing motions with her hands. "You would have been fine. These two would have figured it out."

"It would have taken us longer though and I'm her bloody doctor," groused Jett, not looking too happy with himself. He was unloading our breakfast boxes onto the table. When he opened the lids, the smells that came out were amazing and my mouth started watering. This was going to be one great breakfast.

I settled Lottie on a bench by the table while Julie and Jett were setting stuff out. Julie got the travel mugs and poured coffee for all of us.

"Wow, who packed breakfast?" asked Lottie. "This is so much better than what we usually have from the hotel."

Jett was stuffing his face with what looked like a bacon and egg roll while handing out the remainder for us to unwrap. They were still piping hot, Julie had put them in a cool box as it was insulated. I don't think people realised that you could keep food hot in them as well as cold.

Jett pointed at Julie. "All Julie's doing. She was up at three am this morning cooking. It smelled amazing and all she let me have was one slice of toast," he pouted.

Julie laughed and pushed his finger out of her face. It was a sight to see. I don't think any of us had ever seen her so relaxed.

"You're such a liar! I made you eggs, bacon and toast while this was cooking. If I hadn't stopped you eating, we wouldn't have anything for breakfast."

I watched the two of them tease each other and realised that Jett treated Julie the same way that he treated Lottie, as if she was a much loved younger sister.

"Well, I don't care about Jett starving because this breakfast is awesome, Julie. Thank you for going to the trouble," Lottie said.

Julie shrugged. "It was no trouble. I'm glad that I could do something to make our journey better. And it goes a small way towards saying thanks. Thanks to all of you for giving me a chance of having a different life."

I heard a sniff next to me, then Lottie got up and went over to Julie. Pulling the smaller woman into her arms, she hugged her tight. "You don't have to do anything to thank us. You're quickly becoming an important part of our family. By the time you meet all of us, you may want to run. You've met Jett, right?" She muttered sarcastically. "Well, there are four more just like him out there."

I knew Lottie was trying to lighten the mood and had no problem throwing Jett under the bus.

I sniggered at Jett's irritated, "Hey! I'm awesome and a kick-ass boss!"

Julie laughed and gave Lottie a last hug before moving over to Jett and putting her arm around his waist to give him a sideways hug. Patting his chest, she said, "Don't worry, boss, I got your back. Here, eat another roll, you sound hangry." She shoved another roll at him.

This caused us all to laugh harder. Jett scowled at her. Through a mouth full of roll all we heard was a garbled, "No respect, I tell you."

Julie grinned up at him shamelessly and full out belly laughed when he growled at her. Swatting at him, "You don't scare me," she said through laughter, "My cat is bigger than yours." Her eyes got huge when he roared in her face, then she squealed and took off with Jett chasing her.

Lottie and I were killing ourselves laughing at the two of them chasing each other around the car. Eventually, Jett caught her, but only because she was laughing so much she stopped running. With his arm hooked around her head, he pulled her low and walked her towards us, all the time rubbing her head and talking baby talk to her.

"Nice, kitty, kitty."

Next to me, Lottie snorted with laughter, then turned bright red when I looked at her in surprise.

Shrugging, she said, "Best you find out these things about me now."

I just shook my head at her in amusement, as if her snorting while she laughed would put me off her in any way.

Jett and Julie finally made it back to us. Julie's face was bright red from laughing so hard. Poking Jett in the stomach, she teased him, "You do know that I let you catch me, old man."

Letting her go, Jett looked smug as he bragged to her, "Who are you calling *'old man'*? I caught you before you'd taken five steps."

"I think we need to have a race at the next family meeting," stated Lottie. "My money's on Julie. She can take you, *'old man,'*" she chortled. Her whole face was lit up with laughter. It was a stunning sight.

Jett looked at me shaking his head sadly. "No respect, I tell you, Kyle. Are you sure you want to put up with her disrespectful arse?"

I laughed at him, pulling Lottie closer to me. "Since it's not me they're pulling the piss out of, I think I'm okay, thanks."

Next to me, Lottie was still shaking with laughter at the look on Jett's face. Julie was still beaming. We could see that Jett wasn't upset at all but was simply enjoying the fact that Julie had loosened up enough to have fun.

Clapping her hands at us, Julie started packing up. "Right, how about we pack up and go before it gets too hot. I, for one, am looking forward to seeing where you are all from. Jett, give Lottie her pain pill."

She pointed a finger at Lottie when Lottie started to protest. "No lip from you. Pain pill, snuggle on your male and sleep, in that order. No arguments," she declared firmly, moving off to the vehicle with one of the food boxes.

Lottie's eyes got big at the command and Jett tried hard not to laugh. From the corner of her mouth, she whispered to me, "Julie can be scary when she wants."

"I heard that," came from the other side of the vehicle.

"And apparently she also has ears like a bat," Lottie said in a loud whisper, her voice full of laughter.

Taking the pills that Jett handed to her with a bottle of water, she took them with no further complaint. I could tell from the strain on her face that her head was bothering her.

Walking her back to the vehicle, I helped her in and got in behind her. I put a pillow on my lap and pulled her down so that her head was on the pillow. Considering her height, it wasn't the most comfortable position, but it was still better than leaning up against me or the door. As it was cool in the car with the air-conditioning on, I covered her with the light blanket that Julie had handed me earlier.

Jett and Julie got back in the car after making sure all was secure in the back.

Looking at me in the rear-view mirror, Jett's eyes looked serious. "All good?"

Nodding at him, I replied, "All good."

Putting the car in gear, Jett pulled out onto the road for the final two hours of the journey.

In the back of the car, with Lottie lying quietly in my lap, I took the time to enjoy the peace before we got home to all the responsibilities that awaited me there. Julie and Jett were quietly talking in the front, and the music was on playing the southern rock we all seemed to favour. Playing at the moment was 'Blaze of Somethin' by *A Thousand Horses*. I ran my hand gently over Lottie's head, careful of the scar that was fully healed but still a little sensitive. Her breathing deepened as she fell asleep. Closing my eyes, I felt a sense of peace like I hadn't since I was a child. I hoped that Lottie would be happy living on our small farm and raising her horses there.

CHAPTER 10

LOTTIE

WHYTE'S FARM

Back in the vehicle after the amazing breakfast that Julie had packed, I was still smiling and buzzing from the laughter we'd had at Jett's expense. What the other two didn't realise is that people didn't often get to see this side of Jett. Usually, he was so serious and responsible. A lot of pressure and responsibility was put on him by keeping all the staff and surrounding villagers happy and healthy, as well as those on neighbouring farms. Added to that, he was often called in to cover at the hospital when they needed additional support. Taking Julie on as a nurse was a great idea, if this was how it was going to affect him.

I got as comfortable as I could on the back seat, which was a bit of a feat with my nearly six-foot frame, but I managed. With my head on Kyle's lap and him softly running his fingers over my head, I felt the pain pills kick in and my eyes start to get heavy as I fell to sleep.

It seemed like I had only just been asleep for a minute when I felt Kyle gently running his fingers over my face.

"Angel, you need to wake up. We're nearly there."

I groaned loudly which had them all laughing at me. "That was the best sleep I have had all week and you had to wake me up. Just leave me here," I grumbled, but sat up anyway, rubbing the sleep from my face.

Turning to Kyle, I face planted on his chest, which was rumbling as he tried to hold in his laughter. Looking up at him, I saw his face lit up in amusement. "So mean," I whispered.

"I wanted you to see the farm from the start of our property line," he explained. Sitting up, I took more notice of where we were going. I could see the river to the right of us running alongside the road. Now and then a bird flew down to the water and swooped back up again.

The bush was so green since we'd had some rain, and everything looked clean.

"We're about ten minutes from the main house. The fishponds and tanks will be coming up soon on the right." He pointed out of the window and, sure enough, just ahead I could see large ponds with staff tending them.

Jett continued down the well-maintained dirt road and just ahead I could see the green roof of what I assumed was the main house. To the left, there was what looked like a workshop with storerooms attached. All the buildings were painted white with shiny new galvanised roofs. Big trees surrounded the buildings, providing shade from the relentless sun. Just to the right of the workshop was a paddock with a shelter inside, and behind the paddock a new building was going up.

Tears hit my eyes as I realised what I was seeing. "Oh Kyle," I cried. "You said you had stables."

Jett stopped the vehicle so that I could have a proper look at what my mate had done for me.

Kyle shrugged like it wasn't a big deal to have new stables built. "We did have stables, but they weren't good enough, so I had them torn down and new ones put up. The paddock needed re-doing anyway. I told you, Angel, I want you to be happy, because if you're happy then I'm happy."

By that point I was a blubbering mess, to know that he had gone to so much trouble while I was in the hospital. But it wasn't just him. I knew that his brothers and mother had organised all this at his say-so. They would all be getting massive hugs when I next saw them.

I felt a hand on my knee and looked up to see Jett smiling at me. "You deserve this, Lottie. Everything that you've ever gone through has brought you to this moment, with a male who puts you first and that's how it should be. You're going to have a happy life here, and I'm so grateful to be here to see you live it."

I grabbed the tissue that Julie held out to me. Taking a huge breath in and letting it out slowly, I finally got hold of myself. I squeezed Jett's hand. "Thank you, Jett. I hope one day you find someone that does that for you. That would make me truly happy."

Turning to Kyle, my eyes filled with tears again. I took his face in my hands. "I don't have the words to explain how happy you've made me, Kyle, for doing all this for me and for putting me first in so many ways. From the bottom of my heart, thank you. I promise to do my best to always put you first and be there whenever you need me."

I reached up to press my lips to his in a soft kiss, only to break away when I heard a sob from the front seat. I saw Julie crying and dabbing at her eyes. Jett was rolling his eyes at her, but I could see they were also looking suspiciously wet.

Unfortunately for him, Julie saw him roll his eyes. She smacked him on the arm and faced front with a huff. "What did you hit me for?" he exclaimed.

"For being an arse," groused Julie.

I gave a tear filled giggle at the two of them and Jett winked at me in the rear-view mirror. I knew he'd done it so I'd have time to pull myself together before we got to the main house.

"The girls will bring your horses over next week when the building's finished," explained Kyle.

"Thank you. I'm looking forward to seeing all my babies again," I said softly.

Jett put the vehicle in gear and we carried on down the road towards the main house. We drove up a slight incline and the house was at the top, surrounded by a garden filled with massive trees, plants, and a vast amount of green lawn.

'Wow, this garden is amazing,' I thought to myself.

There was a large, covered veranda with beautiful wooden furniture. All around were hanging baskets and potted plants. I was in awe. Standing on the steps of the veranda, with a wide smile on her face, was Annie. Waving at us she went to where the vehicles parked under a roof to the side of the veranda, Annie was bouncing on her toes as Jett brought the vehicle to a stop. Kyle got out and caught his mother up in a big hug as she came down the steps.

Pressing his forehead to hers, he looked into her eyes and took a deep breath. She reached up and kissed his cheek.

"It's so good to have you home," she said. With one last hug, she moved towards me as I was stepping out of the vehicle.

Soon I was enfolded in her strong arms and pulled into a tight hug. I felt all the stress that I'd been holding onto leaving my body as soon as she took me in her arms.

"Annie," I whispered into her hair.

"Baby girl, welcome home," she whispered back.

Turning from me, she saw Julie waiting quietly by the vehicle, looking unsure.

"You must be Julie." Julie nodded, and Annie moved towards her with her hands out. "Welcome to our home, Julie."

Annie pulled her in for a hug and the look on Julie's face nearly broke my heart. This was another female who'd not had enough love in her life. She sank into Annie and held on tight.

"Thank you for having me, Annie."

The older woman pulled away slightly and looked at Julie with a smile. "You're very welcome, sweetie. Our home is your home."

Jett came around from the other side and threw his arms out wide. "Annie, my love, please tell me you've decided to put me out of my misery and run away with me." He grabbed her up in a laughing hug and swung her around.

I felt Kyle stiffen next to me and I patted his arm. Quietly I said to him, "Relax, they do this with all the older generation ladies. It's just a bit of fun and makes everyone laugh."

True to my words, Annie laughed and swatted at Jett. "You boys are going to do that one day and the lady may just take you up on it," she laughed at him. "Come in and have some tea and sandwiches before you have to leave again. You're welcome to spend the night if you want to."

Jett put one arm around Annie's shoulders, the other around Julie, and escorted them onto the veranda. "Thank you, Annie, but I need to get back today. The clinic is backed up at the moment and it's only another couple of hours drive."

We sat down around the table that had been set with tea and sandwiches. Annie got us caught up with all the goings-on that had happened in the week I was in the hospital. She wasn't expecting Rory, Sean, and Amy back today, as they'd decided to spend the night at a hotel in town.

Once we'd finished eating and talking, Jett left us with instructions on what to do if I wasn't feeling well, and a reminder that I needed to rest as much as possible.

He went on for so long that Julie told him to leave and that she had it under control. "You need to trust that I know my job, Jett. If there's something I can't handle I'll be in touch, thank you very much."

It made us laugh to see her like this. I swear if she'd been in her tiger form, her hair would've been standing up, she was so irritated with him.

After a while, Jett got up to go, so another round of hugs was in order. He waved at us from the vehicle, then pulled away in a cloud of dust.

We all went into the house and Annie showed us where we would be sleeping. She'd had to move everything around during the week and had given Kyle and me the main bedroom with the en suite. I still felt guilty about that, but Annie wasn't having any of it. She'd moved into a room on the other side of the lounge to give us some privacy, and Julie would be in the spare room on that side.

By now I was feeling tired again, so Annie took Julie to her room to get settled, and I was left with strict instructions to get some sleep.

Kyle closed the curtains so that the room was darker and put the overhead fan on to cool it down slightly. I sat on the side of the bed and slipped my shoes off. I didn't have the energy to do much else. Kyle put his hand on my chin and tilted my head up.

"You okay, Angel?" He looked worried.

"Yeah, honey. Just tired. Once I've slept a bit, I'll feel better."

"Let's get you comfortable and into bed then," he said. "Lift your arms, Angel." I raised my arms, and he slipped his hands under my shirt then lifted it off over my head. My eyes were drifting shut as he undid my bra and kissed each of my breasts in turn.

"Beautiful," he breathed.

I felt a shirt being pulled back on over my head and I realised that his scent had gotten stronger, so I opened my eyes and saw that he was now shirtless. He had put me in his shirt, and I was engulfed in his scent. I was annoyed with myself for being so tired that I couldn't appreciate his bare chest. Lifting me, he laid me to the bed and I felt his hands on the button of my shorts, opening them and sliding them down my legs. Turning on my side, I pulled the pillows close. A light cover was pulled up over me and, as I felt myself sink into sleep, I felt a kiss on the back of my head and heard a whispered, "Love you, Angel."

CHAPTER 11

KYLE

We had been back on the farm for nearly two weeks and Lottie was almost back to herself. Her horses had been delivered and were settled in the new stables. Two of her staff members had happily moved along with the horses, as they had family on our farm. The new staff quarters were nearly finished, and the communal kitchen and dining room had gone down well with everyone. Another big change was that we were now starting to find out more about the other families and how they worked together. We learnt that they did a lot of trading with each other, bartering for products that each farm specialised in or produced.

I'd found out about this in the first week that Lottie was with us. Mum had gone to town to pick up stock, and to deliver jams, sauces, and fish to the restaurants and hotels. She'd come back with meat from the butcher in town and Lottie asked why we didn't just ask either the MacGregors or Russos for meat or game in exchange for our fish. We must have looked puzzled, so Lottie and Amy explained that the four families and some of the smaller farms in the surrounding areas exchanged or bartered goods. There was even a website set up to help the process. It was a proper network of produce, services and labour that satisfied everyone, and helped strengthen bonds between the families and their surrounding communities.

It certainly opened my eyes to how isolated we had made ourselves. Amy told me we'd find out more at the next family meeting that was taking place the next weekend at a central point specifically built for this purpose. It wasn't far from The Lake, which was where they'd all been the night the poachers hit us.

I got a call from Jett to say that he'd be stopping in the next day to check on Lottie to see how she was progressing. I told him that she'd been headache-free for approximately thirty-six hours and that she was itching to get back to her horses full time. She was spending a couple of hours every day working them with her staff and was making calls to schedule training for a couple of clients who had troublesome horses.

This wasn't something I'd realised, but from both her sisters and Amy, I discovered that Lottie was one of the best in the country at retraining troublesome horses. She'd set up an office next to the stables and had her sisters bring over all her files and notes. I'd wondered if we needed to build more stables. Lottie hadn't asked or said anything, but I knew she wouldn't. I'd spoken to Renee and she agreed that Lottie wouldn't want to feel like she was taking advantage. Mum and I planned to visit the Moore farm to look at the set up they had there. I was going to make sure that Lottie had all she needed to successfully run her business from our farm.

With Jett coming the next day to hopefully give us the all clear on finally being able to complete our mating bond, I decided to have a chat with Amy and my brothers about what we could do to make it special for Lottie.

We'd just finished lunch and Lottie had gone to lie down for an hour after spending the morning down at the stables. I went over to the cottage on the other side of the garden where they were all sitting on the veranda waiting for me as we'd arranged.

Walking up the steps, I saw they were all grinning at me and that Julie had joined them. I rolled my eyes. "Really! How old are you? Three?"

This just made them laugh more.

Amy was the first to pull herself together.

"Okay, enough you lot. Kyle, tell us what you need. But before we go any further, can I just say thank you for doing this for my friend. Lottie is one of the sweetest people I know and deserves for tomorrow night to be special." This said, she handed me a glass of fresh orange juice as I sat down.

I explained what I wanted to do, and by the time I'd finished, my brothers were silent and Amy was looking at me with soft eyes. She got up, came over to me, and threw her arms around me in a tight hug, Julie joining her. I looked at my brothers who just grinned.

"Leave the heavy stuff to us, brother, we'll get it sorted," reassured Rory.

"Amy and I will sort the food out," said Julie, finally releasing me and moving off to the rail of the veranda. "Is there anything specific you want or are you happy for us to choose?"

"I'm good with you choosing. Amy probably knows Lottie's preferences better than me anyways, as they've known each other longer."

Amy and Julie disappeared into the house, discussing what they would make.

Sean came over to me and laid his forehead against mine with his hand tight on the back of my neck. "So proud of you, Kyle. You've grown into a fantastic male, and I'm proud to call you, my brother."

It was the first time since they'd come home that I truly felt like they were my brothers. I hadn't seen them for over ten years, since they'd been forced to leave us because of their mother. It was great to know they were here for me now, to lean on when I needed to. I pulled him tight into my arms for a hug, not having to say anything. I felt Rory squeeze my shoulder.

"Don't worry about anything for tomorrow. We'll sort it out for you," confirmed Sean.

"Thanks. I wasn't sure how I was going to get everything done by myself without Lottie getting suspicious, and I really want it to be a surprise."

Both Sean and Rory nodded in understanding. "Don't worry, we can sort most of it out, and then you can come check up on what we've set up during the day, although I think Julie and Amy will have sorted all the froufrou stuff out by then," laughed Rory.

Out of the corner of my eye, I saw Sean tap his nose slightly and nod his head towards the main house. Turning, I saw Lottie walking towards us through the garden.

She stopped to chat with the gardener on her way and for the thousandth time, I couldn't believe how lucky I was that she was mine. She was barefoot and had on a pair of shorts, her long legs a golden brown from having been in the sun. Her tight tank top showed off her amazing breasts. The tank was olive green, her favourite colour, and it just made her eyes seem to glow. Her hair was still short on one side and long on the other, but I knew she wanted it cut as soon as her scar was completely healed.

Her whole face lit up as she laughed at something the gardener said. She took the tomato he held out to her and went over to the garden tap to wash it off. I groaned as she bent over. Her long legs were bare and her arse was showcased to perfection. I was adjusting myself in my shorts just as she turned around, catching me in the act. She was laughing at me, her smile beaming out, causing me to groan again.

"Just one more night," I muttered quietly to myself, or maybe not so quietly, as my brothers were laughing at me again.

By now Lottie was at the bottom of the veranda steps. I held out my hand to her, causing her to roll her eyes, but she took it anyway.

"You do know I'm not an invalid anymore," she chided.

I shrugged at her. "Humour me, Angel. I can't help worrying about you. I may let up in about fifty years or so."

This comment caused her to roll her eyes so hard I thought they might fall out of her head.

I turned her round and pulled her to me, wrapping my arms around her just below her breasts. Leaning back against me, she tilted her head back to kiss my chin.

"So, what were you all up to over here?" she questioned, her eyebrows raised.

Sean and Rory just shrugged and sat back down. "Just talking about work, seeing if Kyle needs a hand with anything over the next week."

Just then Amy and Julie came back out with trays of drinks and snacks. I knew Amy must have heard us. She was a Wild Dog Shifter, so her hearing was phenomenal.

Lottie stared at the pile of sandwiches, crisps and fruit on the table. "We just had lunch an hour ago," she said.

Amy just shrugged. "My males are always hungry," she said, reaching for a sandwich. This made us all laugh.

"Okay, not just my males," she grinned, then gave a small squeak as Sean grabbed her and pulled her onto his lap. Adjusting her so that she was comfortable, Rory pulled her feet up onto his lap.

I heard Julie snort, and turned to see her watching this, her head tilted to one side. "Huh, arranging your mates to your liking must be a Whyte family thing," she stated with a shrug, reaching for a sandwich before plunking herself down on the swing and set it rocking slightly.

I guessed we were having a second lunch, not that I minded. I could always eat, and sitting here in the company of friends, brothers, and Lottie, I felt totally at ease for the first time in a long time.

From the garden, we heard my mother's voice. "What are you all doing over here?" she asked, her voice getting louder as she came closer.

"Having a second lunch," I drawled.

"Did I not make enough lunch?" she said, looking at us in concern.

"You made plenty, Annie," said Julie. "This lot are just bottomless pits, although I must say it's nice not to be hungry anymore." She suddenly stopped talking, looking guilty.

I wanted to kill Julie's family when she let slip things like this. How they didn't see what an amazing female she was escaped me. I knew my family felt the same.

"Oh, honey." My mother's face was soft as she sat down next to Julie and pulled her into her arms.

Julie had quickly become one of my mother's favourite people and I didn't see her letting go easily. My brothers and I were in agreement about keeping her here with us as long as possible. As it was, we were already making plans to have additional bathrooms added to the house and a small clinic built here for her and Jett. It made sense for us to have one here and I would soon speak to the other families and suggest that they all build some sort of medical facility on their properties. This would save us all having to set up a makeshift one every time it was needed.

"I didn't mean to make you sad, Annie. This is the happiest I have been in my entire life. This is what family is meant to be, isn't it?" she asked, closing her eyes.

My mother's eyes were bright with unshed tears as she blinked rapidly, and

I saw Amy and Lottie's eyes show the same emotion. Lottie stuck her face into my neck, and breathed hard, trying to keep control. My mother had Julie tucked into her body and was running her hand through Julie's hair.

Mum gave a deep sigh and pressed a kiss to Julie's forehead. "Yes, baby girl, this is what family is. And you never have to worry about not having a family, because you'll always have a home here."

We were all quiet for a bit and I could see my brothers' bodies were tense and their eyes flared with anger. Amy was running her hands over both of them soothingly. Then I became aware that Lottie was repeatedly patting my chest and running her hand through my hair.

Taking a deep breath, I released it slowly, the rage that had been building inside me gradually easing. Giving Lottie one last hug, I went over to Julie and my mother. Crouching on the floor next to them, I saw that Julie still had her eyes closed and her face was wet with tears. She started when I touched her hand and her eyes flew open. Her blue eyes were bright through her tears. I stood her up and hugged her tight. When I let go, I took her head in my hands and looked into her eyes.

"You don't ever have to worry about anything, Julie. You have a home here on this farm for as long as you want to stay. And if you don't want to go with Jett once he says it's safe, you don't have to. We're your family now. If Annie had given me a sister, I would have wanted her to be just like you. You may not be blood, but you are in our hearts. You're my sister and my mother's daughter."

Feeling my brothers come up behind me, I let her go and Rory took her from me into his arms. His voice was a guttural growl, still steeped in anger. "You have three older brothers now, and no one is going to mess with you, trust me. Let your biological family come and see what's waiting for them if they try to take you away."

He passed her on to Sean. "I stand by everything my brothers have said. You're one of the best people I know. You are safe and loved by us, and you never have to leave if you don't want to."

Mum came up next to me and slipped her arms around me. Sean shuffled Julie over to my mother and me not letting her go, we surrounded her and before long Julie was at the centre of a Whyte family hug.

From beside me came a slight sob, and I looked up to see Amy and Lottie, arms around each other, watching us with tears in their eyes. Lifting my arm from around my mother, I motioned for them to come closer. They rushed to us and squirmed their way into the middle of the huddle, which made us all laugh, breaking the tension a little.

As we stood there in that huddle, I couldn't help but feel proud and thankful for the family that I had been born into. That there were families out there that treated their own like trash because of the colour of their fur, or how they looked, was beyond me.

"And that, honey, is why I love you," stated Lottie.

I looked down at her, and then around at my family.

"I said that out loud, didn't I?"

My mother laughed. "That you did, love, that you did. Glad to see some things stay the same. You always talked out loud like that when you were younger. It was how I found out all your secrets. Now if only your brothers had done it too, my life would have been much simpler."

As almost all the chores were done for the day, we all agreed that we'd take the afternoon off and just spend time with each other. It ended up being one of the best family days we'd had since my brothers got back. We were slowly getting back to how it had been before they'd left to join the military. I could tell that Mum was happy that we were settling back into the teasing sibling rivalry we'd always had.

Later that night, lying in bed with Lottie lying against me, her head on my shoulder and one leg thrown over my hips, I felt a contentment like I hadn't felt since my late teens. I hoped that Jett had good news for Lottie tomorrow, and that she'd like the surprise that I'd arranged for her.

CHAPTER 12

LOTTIE

I woke slowly. It was just starting to get light and the room was lovely and cool with a slight breeze making the curtains flutter. It smelled like we'd had a light sprinkling of rain during the night.

Kyle was still asleep next to me, sprawled on his stomach with his arm under his head and his broad back facing towards me, the sheet just covering the top of his very fine arse. My fingers itched to lower that sheet, but I knew that I couldn't start anything that he wouldn't finish. Kyle was adamant we wait to take our mating further until we get the all-clear from Jett, no matter how many times I told him that I feel fine.

Turning away from all the fineness that was my male, I lost myself in thought.

Yesterday afternoon had been emotional, and I'd felt bad for Julie, it hurt to think that her family could be so callous. I hoped she understood that she never had to go back to them as we were her family now.

I knew how much having a family that loved you unconditionally affected how you saw yourself. I knew if I hadn't had my grandmother and my sisters growing up, I'd be a very different person today. I was looking forward to seeing them tomorrow at the local family meeting. Usually, it was just one or two from each family that attended, but as this was the Whytes' first meeting it had been decided that everyone would attend. I was certainly hoping that Jett would give me the all-clear today, as it was getting harder and harder to deny the bond between Kyle and me.

Feeling cold air brush against my breasts, my eyes popped open to see Kyle leaning up on one elbow. His eyes were on my breasts as they lay uncovered to his gaze since he had removed the sheet. Lifting his hand, he circled my nipples with his finger causing them to shrink and pull into tight buds. At my slight moan, his eyes lifted to mine. They were dark with need as they went back to staring at my breasts. Lowering his head, he sucked one into his mouth. I moaned again, "Kyle."

Every time he tugged on my breast, my hips lifted involuntarily, and I knew that if I put my hand on myself, I would be wet. Kyle pushed the sheet further down my body until I was laid completely bare to his gaze. My breath shuddered through me. I was so turned on that I knew that it would take just a small brush on my clit to get me to combust.

Kissing his way between my globes, he moved on to my other breast, first sucking the nipple deep into his mouth before letting go with a pop, then blowing gently on it. Looking at me with heavily lidded eyes, he kept on doing this. By now I was squirming on the bed, and he still hadn't said anything.

He held me down by putting his arm across my hips just above my pussy and repeated his ministrations on my breasts until they were aching. I was panting hard and flooded with need. My body seemed to be moving on its own. I'd never felt like this with anyone else. It felt like I could explode any minute.

Finally, when I was close to sobbing with need, I felt his hand at my pussy, just over my clit. He flicked it quickly and I was gone. Stars burst behind my eyes as I keened in pleasure and pushed my fists onto the headboard behind my head.

I'm not sure how long I came for, but it seemed to go on forever in rolling waves. When I finally came down, Kyle was looking at me smugly.

"Morning, Angel. Sleep well?"

I just huffed at him as I had no energy for a proper reply. Reaching for him, I circled him with my arms and just hung on until I felt able to speak coherently.

"Oh my god, Kyle, that was amazing, but I thought we were waiting to get the all-clear?"

He smiled down at me. "We won't be doing anything else this morning until Jett clears you for full activity, but I know you're going to pass your physical with flying colours. This was just a preview of what's to come this evening."

'If that was the preview I may very well die from orgasms. I wonder if that's possible,' I thought.

Kyle's big body started shaking with laughter, his hard cock pushing against me. I realised that I'd spoken that thought out loud.

His eyes were full of mirth. "I don't think it's possible to die from orgasms, babe, but if it is, what a way to go!" He was full-on laughing at me now as I felt myself flush red with embarrassment.

"God, I love you. Don't ever change, Angel," he said, when he'd finally stopped laughing.

He seemed content to just hold me, even with his cock still hard between us. I tentatively moved my body causing him to groan with need.

"Kyle, let me. You haven't let me touch you since that first morning in the hospital."

"I can't, Lottie. I don't want to hurt you, and I know with you I'm not going to be able to hold back."

"Okay, so we don't mate fully, but I can still do other things. I won't move my head from my pillow, and you can do all the work," I said, nodding my head towards my breasts, hoping he would get it without me having to say anything.

I saw the moment he understood what I was saying, because his eyes darkened with heat and his voice came out in a growl. "Angel, are you saying you want me to fuck your breasts?"

I could feel myself flushing from the top of my head down to my toes. Kyle pushed himself up looking down at me.

"You are so fucking beautiful, Angel." He ran a finger down my chest towards my stomach. "Look at you, all flushed. So gorgeous."

He lifted his eyes to mine, looking at me from under his lids. I started to squirm under him. He was now kneeling with his legs either side of me just above my pelvis. His cock was big and hard, pointing up towards his belly button. His muscular stomach rippled when he grabbed hold of his cock and squeezed it. Pre-cum dripped from the head and I licked my lips, panting slightly, wanting to taste him.

Kyle groaned as he moved up the bed towards my head. Leaning over, he grabbed the massage oil he'd used to massage my back and shoulders. This had been a great help with my headaches. After drizzling some oil on my breasts, he closed the bottle, then proceeded to rub the oil over my globes, twisting my nipples as he did so. Finally, when I couldn't take it anymore, he grabbed my hands and put them on my breasts. "Hold them for me, Angel. Last chance. Are you sure you're up for this?"

"Please, Kyle, don't deny me now."

He pushed his hard cock between my globes and started moving. Every time his cock came close to my mouth, I licked the head, hungry for the taste. Finally, lifting my head, I took his entire head into my mouth. Kyle cursed and put his hands on my head, holding me still and supporting my head. I lifted my eyes to see him looking down at me, his face tense with need. Then he semi-shifted as sometimes happened when his gorilla was making himself known, and his whole body shuddered as ropes of cum shot out of him. I took what I could and the rest painted my breasts and chest. Kyle was shuddering over me as he finished. He rubbed his cum across my breasts marking me.

Breathing deeply, he lay his body over mine, careful to keep his full weight off me. I ran my hands over his back gently while he came down.

"What happened to not moving your head?" he growled at me, looking annoyed.

I shrugged. "I tried, but my mate is so hot."

He just grunted and buried his head into my neck and shoulder, still breathing heavily. With a sigh, he lifted himself off me and rolled over on to the bed before standing up and stretching.

Bending and scooping me off the bed into his arms, he said, "Come on, pretty girl, let's shower. We have lots to do today."

I was confused as to what we had going on today that was different from any other day.

"What do we have going on today, other than Jett coming over?" I questioned.

"Once Jett has been, I have arranged for your sisters to come over and spend the day, so all you females can have a girl's day. You'll get a manicure, a pedicure, and they'll do your hair for you. Unfortunately, Reggie can't make it."

I felt tears well in my eyes. This male always seemed to make me cry with all that he did for me.

"What about Annie? Isn't she joining us?"

Kyle smiled gently down at me as he put me in the shower and started the water. "I love that you thought of my mum. She wanted to join you but has already got something going on that she can't get out of."

I nodded. Reaching up, I kissed him. "Thank you for arranging this for me. I'm so looking forward to seeing my sisters."

"Anything for you, Angel," he said, reaching for the soap and loofah and started to wash me.

Once we were done in the shower, we dressed and went hand-in-hand to the kitchen, looking for coffee. I knew Annie would have been up for a while already, even though it wasn't even six-thirty yet.

Each of us grabbed a cup of our coffee, we went out to the couch on the back veranda. Kyle sat down and pulled me onto his lap, arranging me as he wanted me before picking up his coffee and taking a long swallow. I had gotten used to him doing this, but it still sent a shot of amusement through me every time. I just shrugged and drank my coffee, looking out of the garden and enjoying the peace of the new morning. The sun was almost completely up by now and its light was shining through the raindrops that were clinging to the plants. I knew it was going to be another hot day.

Rory, Sean,and Amy came out of their little house with their coffee and took a seat on their couch on their veranda. Kyle raised a hand as they sat down and arranged Amy over them to their satisfaction. I caught her eye and smirked. She just shrugged her shoulders and lifted her hands as if to say, *'What can you do?'*

We all sat there quietly drinking our coffee until we heard Julie and Annie in the kitchen starting breakfast. Amy and I both got up. Grabbing our cups, I leant over and kissed Kyle. After one last kiss and running my hand through Kyle's hair, I went to the kitchen to help get breakfast together for all of us.

Once Amy came in, Annie gave us each a job. Julie had made more coffee, and gave each of us a second cup before taking some out to her brothers on the veranda.

There was a lot of laughing and chatting while we got breakfast ready. We could hear the males out on the veranda talking over what was happening today. I knew if we asked them to help with breakfast, they would, but I enjoyed this time of bonding with the other females in my life. I could tell they felt the same way.

Breakfast was the usual loud affair of teasing, laughing, and talking about what was expected workwise during the day.

Once breakfast was done and we were sitting around the huge kitchen table, I asked Annie why none of the chairs matched. She explained that they were all made by Rory, and each one showed how he'd improved over the years. The first chair he'd made, when he was twelve, was in the corner of the kitchen. It held a basket full of odds and ends of material as Rory claimed it was unsafe to sit on.

His most recent was the one he'd made since he had returned home. This was at the head of the table and it was Annie's seat. It was so beautiful, almost like a throne, with elegant scroll work on the arms and a plush velvet fabric seat. Looking closely at the carvings, you could see that they were gorillas in various poses. It was really something to see.

Amy and Julie were so excited to have a girl's day and made no bones about hurrying the males out of the house once breakfast was done.

"Anybody would think you don't love us," Sean grumbled at Amy.

She just rolled her eyes. "I love you, babe, but you are seriously cramping my style. Go and beat something up, preferably not your brother, as I have plans for you two later."

"Eww, my ears, my ears," cringed Julie, shuddering in disgust. "I do not need to hear about what my brothers are like in bed."

This made us all crack up with laughter.

"And I certainly don't want to know what my baby boys are up to," stated Annie, who was making her way out to her shed. "They're all still virgins and my grandbabies will be delivered by a stork, no shenanigans necessary," she shouted from the corridor.

The looks on the twins' faces were priceless.

Kyle grabbed me and kissed the socks off me, leaving me breathless. Then, with a slap on my arse, he turned to leave but not before ruffling Julie's hair, messing it up. She growled and swatted at him only to have Sean and Rory do the same thing. She finally snapped and roared at them as they left, laughing the whole way out the back door.

Once we had all calmed down, we made a plan on what was needed for our pamper day. I was really excited about spending time with all of them.

Julie was in charge of food as she was the best cook. She said she would make enough for the males. Amy said she would get together some drinks and put a cool box on the veranda so we wouldn't have to move from there. My job was to see Jett and get the all-clear, then come back and spend time with my sisters.

I really loved these women and couldn't help but feel grateful that they were in my life.

CHAPTER 13

KYLE

After a relaxing start to the day, we left the women laughing at us for hassling Julie so much she roared at us. Rory, Sean, and I left the kitchen feeling like our job teasing our new sister was done. I'd forgotten how good it was to spend time with my brothers.

We went over to the workshops to catch up with the foreman on what needed to be done that day since the three of us would be out of contact for most of it. Once the staff meeting was over, it was just the three of us left.

Rory slapped me hard on the shoulder and gave me a big grin. "Are you ready to get this day going, little brother?"

"Yeah, let me bring the Land Rover and trailer over and we can get it loaded up. Did you manage to get the mosquito nets and bedding out here?"

They both nodded. "We brought all that out here last night, once you guys had gone to bed. We needed to change and go for a run anyway."

"Thanks. I know I don't say this often enough, but I'm so glad you guys are home."

They both nodded at me and we became quiet for a moment. Clearing his throat, Sean went to the workshop doors and unlocked them. They had piled the mattress and bedding close to the doors for easy access.

Walking to the garage attached to the workshop, I jumped into the Land Rover with the attached trailer and reversed it as close as I could to the workshop doors.

We made quick work of loading the stuff into the back of the vehicle, including a bed frame that Rory insisted I take.

"I can't have your lady sleeping on the floor, Kyle. This is just a rough one, the wood has too many knots for me to be able to sell it. I was going to offer it to the Russos for one of the chalets at The Lake."

Nodding, I gripped his shoulder. "Thank you, brother."

Sean laughed, then said, "Besides, this way we'll know if it'll hold up to vigorous sleepers," he said, smirking at me.

I shook my head at him and got into the Land Rover. Leaning my head out the window, I said "Well, are you two coming or not?"

"Shotgun," shouted Sean, making me laugh. He was the quieter of the twins, so it wasn't often he beat Rory to the punch.

The look on Rory's face was priceless.

"You fucker, I can't believe you stuck me with riding in the back."

"Don't worry, Princess," I chuckled. "I'll make sure to drive slowly so you don't bruise your sensitive arse going over the bumps."

Grumbling about unworthy, ungrateful brothers, Rory jumped into the back of the Land Rover. When I heard him hit the roof of the cab, I took off. Sean was still laughing next to me.

Looking at him from the corner of my eye, I asked, "So what brought that on?" I knew that Rory must have done something to annoy Sean this morning and this was a form of punishment. It was how the two of them worked.

Sean smiled wickedly at me. "He finished the coffee this morning and didn't make a second pot, so when Amy wanted a cup there was none. Instead of them coming back to bed, I had to listen to her chew him out. For someone so small, she can get mean when you mess with her coffee. So not only did I miss out on time in bed with our mate, but I had to listen to the two of them bicker while the coffee was brewing. He deserves to eat dust."

I laughed at his disgruntled tone and made a note to never come between my mate and her coffee.

The drive didn't take long since the spot we were going to was only a few miles away.

Pulling up under the trees, I took in the place where Lottie and I would be spending the evening. It was by a natural hot spring and, when we were younger, my father had built a flat concrete area to sit on and installed a number of steel posts so a big cover could be put up. This was where I was planning to put the bed for the night. He'd also built a fire pit so we wouldn't have to worry about bush fires in the dry season. Dad never liked building a fire on the bush floor.

The plants around the hot spring were lush and green, with big ferns and grasses swaying in the slight breeze.

We jumped out of the Land Rover and started unloading. First, we put the bed together and laid the mattress on it, then Rory brought the tarpaulin out. We tied this to the steel posts above the bed. If it rained tonight, hopefully we should stay dry.

I made the bed up with the bedding that Amy had packed. There was a beautiful bedspread in blues, greens and browns, covered in embroidered figures of elephants and gorillas. In the middle, LOTTIE and KYLE were stitched in big letters. I traced over them with my finger. I could tell a lot of work had gone into this. I was both amazed and touched by the effort and thought that had gone into it.

While I was putting the bed together and admiring the bedspread, my brothers had been busy putting up the fairy lights around the bottom of the tarpaulin and checking the batteries. I knew it would look fantastic once the sun had set.

"Where did you have this made?" I asked them. They looked at the bedspread laid out over the bed and their faces softened.

Looking at each other, they smiled. "So that was why she came to bed so late last night and likely why she was so grumpy this morning," commented Rory.

Sean rolled his eyes, but then he looked at the bedspread again and smiled. "Amy's been working on this non-stop since the night we brought Lottie home. She said she started embroidery as a way to quiet her mind and de-stress, but I think this might have had the opposite effect," he chuckled. "I know she was working on it late last night but didn't realise she'd finished it."

Running my hand gently over the fabric, I looked again and saw that all the local shifter family names had been added in various places. You wouldn't see them unless you studied the bedspread closely.

My heart filled with love for my brothers' mate, and I felt guilty that I hadn't tried to get to know her better. I made up my mind that I'd rectify that as soon as I could.

Clearing my throat, I looked at my brothers who were still staring at the bedspread in awe.

"I'll make sure Amy knows this is appreciated, and I'll make an effort to get to know her better, because I can tell from this that she's a female who values family."

They nodded at me, then they both tensed and tilted their heads, listening. In the distance, I heard what sounded like one of the quad bikes.

Looking at my watch, I saw that it was already lunchtime and wondered why someone was driving out to find us. Was there some kind of problem back at the farm?

As the quad bike came closer, I saw that it was Amy with Julie sitting behind her. They were pulling one of the small trailers behind the bike. It looked like it was filled with a cool box and a water butt.

They both had huge grins on their faces, so I knew there was nothing to worry about. They pulled up in the shade of the trees.

Switching it off, Amy jumped off the bike and straight into Sean's arms, shouting, "Hello, my gorgeous mate. I missed you so much. We, brought you lunch!"

He shook his head at her exuberance, then gave her a long kiss before passing her over to Rory who gave her the same treatment.

I helped Julie get the cool boxes and water out of the trailer. Julie was smiling from ear to ear, bouncing around on her toes. Clearly, she had something important to say. Eventually she spoke, and it was just what I'd been aching to hear.

"Jett's come and gone, and Lottie got the all-clear. She's having the time of her life with her sisters. We left them catching up on the veranda, painting each other's nails and doing other girly things. I told them we'd be back in an hour or so as Amy and I had something to do for Annie," she babbled, her eyes sparkling with happiness. It was a good look on my new sister. There was such a difference in her since we'd brought her home. Most of her shyness and timidity had vanished.

I gave her a hug and a kiss on the top of her head.

"That's the best news you could have given me, although I knew she would pass with flying colours. Come and see what Amy made for Lottie and me."

Grabbing her by her hand I took her over to the bed and showed her the bedspread. She gasped and clasped her hands together. "Oh, Kyle, that's beautiful. I didn't know that Amy could do work like this." Running her hands gently over our names, I saw her tear up, then her breath hitched when she found her name in the embroidery, right under Annie's.

I put my arm around her and squeezed. "I know. I felt the same way when I saw it."

Turning, I saw that Rory had finally put his mate back down. She had one arm around each of my brothers, a huge smile on her face that showed her dimples. Her brown eyes shone with happiness.

"Do you like it?" she asked, motioning to the bedspread.

I grabbed her up in a hug and swung her around, then put her back down between my brothers.

Holding on to her shoulder, I planted a kiss on her cheek. "I love it, Amy. Thank you. It's beautiful."

"I'm glad you like it. I haven't done something that big before. I'm working on one for your mum at the moment."

Sean and Rory looked surprised at this news and their faces softened as they looked down at Amy.

"She'll love it," I assured her.

"Come eat, you guys," called Julie. I turned to see her setting out chairs around a foldable table that had plenty of food on it.

"I think your thing is to feed people, Julie." I grinned at her, grabbing a sandwich off the pile.

She shrugged her shoulders. "Maybe," she acknowledged. "I like to make people happy, and food makes me happy, so I figured it would make you all happy."

I smiled at her and shook my head. I knew this stemmed from her biological family, but I didn't want to make her uncomfortable by bringing it up.

We all found a place to sit while we ate. It was peaceful and cool under the trees. I couldn't stop looking at the bed covered by the beautiful bedspread, the whole thing under the protective tarpaulin. Sean and Rory had wrapped the fairy lights around the steel poles and across the underside of the tarpaulin so that the whole area was covered in magical sparkling lights. All that was left was for me to put up a mosquito net and we'd be done.

"Do you think I can go for a dip before we go home?" Julie asked.

"I don't see why not," I said.

She jumped up excitedly and went behind the Land Rover. I thought she was going to get changed because I saw her throwing her clothes over the back of the vehicle. But she wasn't changing, she was shifting. I can tell you, when you see a white tiger coming towards you, it doesn't matter that you know it's your sister, you still jump up in fright and run.

The only one who didn't was Amy. She was rolling on the floor laughing at her mates that were part shifted and standing guard over her.

Julie walked over and nuzzled Amy with her head, getting Amy to put her arms around her for a tiger hug.

Now that the flight or fight response had calmed down, I saw Sean was bent over with his hands on his knees.

"Fuuuuck, Julie, can you give us a warning next time?" he panted. "And you, babe!" he exclaimed, pointing at Amy. "Spanking tonight for you for not warning us." Rory nodded in agreement. Amy didn't look concerned at all, just carried on hugging Julie and laughing.

Julie tilted her head to one side as she looked at me. Kneeling, I waited for her to come over. She wasn't small in this form and would have reached to my thighs if I'd been standing up. Her coat was snow white with black stripes, but her eyes were still the same purple-blue.

She nudged her head against my face, so I put my arms around her and hugged her the same as Amy had done. Clearly, she was introducing herself to us, and I knew she'd soon do it again for Mum, and eventually all the families. A deep rumbling purr came from deep inside her.

After my introduction, she went over to my brothers and took her time getting hugs from them. Once she was done, she padded over to the hot springs and took a dip. Looking at her face, I could swear she was laughing at us.

The four of us settled down to watch her playing in the water. Turning to Amy, I asked, "Has Julie been to the springs before today?"

She nodded, grinning. "Yeah, your mum asked her last week if her tiger liked to swim, then told her how to get here. She's something, isn't she?" She looked at me, concern on her face. "We're going to keep her safe, aren't we?"

"She certainly is something," I agreed.

"And yes, we will keep her safe," said Sean, as serious as I'd ever seen him.

CHAPTER 14

LOTTIE

After the males left, we made plans on who'd make what food, then gathered towels, nail polish, face masks and cleansers and took it all to the veranda to wait on my sisters and Jett, who'd sent a message that he was only half an hour away.

I loved sitting on the veranda, drinking coffee and chatting with Julie and Amy, finding out what was happening in their lives. Amy and I were telling Julie stories about things we'd done as kids and explaining who everyone was.

Just as we were about to get up for another coffee, we saw Jett's Landcruiser coming up the hill towards the house. Julie wanted to show him the small clinic that the Whytes were building for her. I knew she didn't want to leave the farm but felt like she owed Jett for getting her away from her family. I tried to explain to her that Jett wouldn't mind if she wanted to stay, but she'd packed her bags so she was ready if he wanted her to leave today. I planned to talk to him during my physical to see what he had to say and give him a heads up.

Jett pulled up, got out of the car and, grabbing his medical bag out of the back, bounded up the stairs wearing his familiar smile. Jett had always been one of my favourite MacGregor brothers.

"Well, look at you three beautiful ladies. I'm loving this welcoming committee," he declared, as he made it to the top of the stairs. He pulled all three of us into a hug at one time, dropping kisses on the tops of our heads.

Amy and I shook our heads laughing at him. We were used to the way he treated us.

Julie still looked a little unsure. "What's up, Buttercup?" he asked.

I could see the indecision on her face, finally, she shook her head. "Nothing," she said awkwardly.

Jett's face bore a look of confusion. I grabbed his arm gently and shook my head at him.

Out loud, I asked, "Do you want coffee or something to eat, or are we going straight to my examination?"

He grinned at me, wriggling his eyebrows. "Someone is in a hurry."

I hit him on the shoulder. "Just you wait until you find your mate, Jett. I'm going to remind you of this little conversation then," I replied.

"Okay, Lotts, I get it. Let's get this over and done with so you can go find your mate and jump his bones," he said, laughing as he strode into the house.

Rolling my eyes, I took him to the bedroom Kyle and I shared.

Once Jett had finished my exam and given me the all-clear, I asked if I could talk to him about something else.

"Jett, before you go, can we chat about Julie?"

He stopped packing up his medical bag and turned to me. He sighed and ran his hand through his hair. Then, resting his hands on his hips, he looked at me with a serious face. "She doesn't want to leave, does she?"

I shook my head. "I'm sorry, Jett. I know you're desperate to have a nurse, but I don't think Julie is it. Annie and the boys have adopted her into their family. They've bonded and now consider her their daughter and sister. She's torn because she feels a strong loyalty to you, but she has finally found a family that loves her just for being her.

"It's not all bad though," I continued, "Because they've started building her a clinic here, somewhere she can do basic first aid and medical care. I think this is a really good thing and, at the next family meeting, I'm going to suggest that each family should build a clinic on their property, all with the same equipment, so you don't need to carry so much stuff around. Julie can handle the one here as well as at the Landry's, as we border each other. Then, when you get a nurse, you could handle your ranch and the Russos. That just leaves my sisters having to find someone to handle theirs. It leaves you free to travel between all the properties if we need you for more serious cases, or you could do a major clinic once a month or so. All this should be easier once we have pilots and a helicopter."

I finally finished my long spiel, taking a deep breath, hoping that Jett could see the benefits of having clinics on each property. He was looking at me silently, but I knew him, and could see he was thinking things over. I watched as his eyes flickered and changed. I knew it was his leopard when I saw the gold in his eyes, but then they went back to their normal brandy colour.

He nodded as if he had made up his mind. "You're right, Lottie, and I can see you've thought this out. Have you mentioned any of this to anyone else?"

I shook my head. "No, I wanted to chat with you first to see if it could work this way. Honestly, the more Julie lets slip about her family, the more I worry about her."

"They don't know where she is, however, they've been searching. I had a call from them last week, as she was seen leaving the hospital with me one evening. I didn't lie when I said I hadn't seen her since the last time I saw her," he grinned.

I snorted with laughter. "Sneaky. Luckily, Kyle's family isn't well known, so she's safe here. Annie, Sean, Rory and Amy go out every night and do a perimeter check. At the next meeting, we should let the Russo's know about her situation. Since they are the only ones who don't know about her, they can keep an eye out and not get caught unawares if they're contacted."

"Yeah, I agree. Honestly, I agree with all you've laid out. Staffed clinics on each property would be a big help, especially when it comes to inoculations and basic first aid. That could take a lot of pressure off me. I'll get Julie to show me the clinic being built here and put her mind at rest about staying on, if that's what she wants."

I gave him a hug. "You're a good male, Jett. Thank you for looking after us and for caring so much."

Returning my hug, he replied, "We're all family, Lottie, and I'll do anything for my family. Now, I hear your sisters on the veranda. Let's go and let them know that you'll live," he added, cheerfully.

CHAPTER 15

KYLE

We spent another couple of hours by the hot springs, putting the last touches to the bed, setting wood into the fire pit, and letting Julie have her fill with swimming in the hot springs. It made us laugh how she splashed around. She finally got out and came over to where we were sitting around the fire pit, waiting for her. Sean and Rory had dozed off and were leaning back against a log. Julie turned her head toward Amy, who was sitting between the twins. She made a chuffing noise and motioned Amy to come over to where I was sitting.

Amy got up slowly and, carefully, came over to sit down next to me. We watched in amusement as Julie went to Rory and Sean and quietly stood over them. I could see Sean was awake but wasn't about to spoil the fun. Without warning Julie flopped down on the twins and proceeded to rub her wet fur all over them. This made Rory groan irritably, which made us all laugh. When she felt she'd tortured them enough, she left them dripping wet.

With her mouth, she took the towel Amy was holding out to her, then sauntered back to the vehicle to get dressed. Rory and Sean moaned good-naturedly about annoying little sisters, making her chortle with laughter. It was good to see her smiling at us, her face clear of the worry that had been clouding it until a couple of days ago. It seemed that as soon as she knew she had a family to count on, she started relaxing and letting us see this happy and mischievous Julie, still gentle and kind but a little mischievous.

We left just as the sun started getting low in the sky. Amy decided to ride back in the Land Rover, as the three of them would fit in the front, so Julie and I took the quad bike. It had been a great afternoon spent with family, and I was looking forward to spending the evening with Lottie.

When we got to the house, Lottie was saying goodbye to her sisters as if she would never see them again. They were in a huddle on the veranda, arms around each other.

I moved through the huddle and encircled Lottie with my arms, hugging her to me and pulling her gently away from her sisters. I softly rubbed the tears from her cheeks and dropped a kiss on her mouth. Taking a step back, I took in her newly shaved hair. She'd finally done it. It made me a bit sad, but I knew it would grow back soon enough. In the meantime, the shortness made her green eyes pop and her face seemed more delicate. Dropping my face into her neck, I took a deep breath. This made her laugh, which had been my aim.

"Did you just sniff me?" she asked.

"Angel, not sure what you ladies have been up to, but you smell amazing." I lowered my head for another sniff.

Turning quickly, I grabbed Ava and Marie and made as if to smell them too.

"Eww, no way are you sniffing me, you overgrown ape," laughed Marie, pushing me away.

I pouted. "Overgrown ape. Really? That's all you could come up with?" I grinned at her.

Laughing at me, Renee grabbed Lottie for a last hug. "We'll see you tomorrow at the meeting. Don't be late!"

Mock saluting, Lottie stood to attention. "Yes, ma'am!"

The sisters finally made their way to the waiting vehicle and started getting in. I called out to them as they were about to leave. "Renee!"

She looked at me out of the driver's window, her brow raised in query.

"Make sure you call my mum when you get home so we know you're safe." Lottie's arm tightened around my waist, as she saw the surprise on Renee's face at this request.

Renee nodded, then blew a kiss to Lottie before putting the vehicle into gear and slowly driving away. We waited until they were out of sight before I turned to Lottie. She was looking at me with soft loving eyes.

"I love that you care about my family, Kyle. We're so used to only depending on each other, that sometimes it comes as a bit of a shock when someone else shows they care."

I shrugged. "They're family, and we always look out for family, blood or not."

Standing on tiptoe, she pressed her lips to mine. Opening my mouth, I deepened our kiss. Then someone cleared their throat and we broke apart. Julie was standing there, a cool box in one hand and a basket in the other.

She was grinning at us, her face full of laughter.

"Thought I'd better stop you before you put on a show," she giggled.

Clearing her throat again, and trying to look serious, she handed me the cool box and basket.

"Food and drinks are in these. I've already put a change of clothes in the trailer." With that, she turned and walked back into the house.

Lottie looked at me with big eyes. "Where are we going?"

"It's a surprise," I murmured, running my hand gently over her shorn head, loving the feel of it under my fingers. She gently nuzzled into my hand, making me groan. I was rock hard at this point and ready to get on to the rest of what I'd planned for our evening.

I put the basket and cool box into the trailer alongside the small bag of clothing. I helped Lottie onto the quad bike, and then started it up. We pulled away from the house into the growing dusk. This was perfect timing. I knew that when we arrived at the hot springs, the combination of twilight and fairy lights would create the perfect romantic atmosphere.

We passed Sean, Amy and Rory coming back from the workshop and waved at them. Amy cupped her hands and shouted at us as we rode past.

"Have fun, but don't be late tomorrow." Then she squealed and Lottie laughed as we watched in the side mirror as Rory threw her over his shoulder.

As we came up to the hot springs, I saw that my plan had worked. The lights were flickering gently in the cooling breeze, and the whole scene was perfect.

I parked and we just sat there for a moment, taking it in. The fairy lights lit the bed, showing off the beautiful bedspread, and to the side, there was a table set with two chairs. I realised that the others had come back and done this. There was a tealight in a glass bottle, and flowers in a vase set in the middle of the table which was laid with plates and cutlery. They'd also strung more lights through the trees, it looked stunning in the twilight.

Behind me, I heard Lottie catch her breath. "Kyle, this is beautiful. Is this what you were doing today?"

"Not just me. Rory, Sean, Amy, and Julie helped. Rory literally made the bed," I chuckled.

She got off the bike and went over to the bed. Moving the mosquito net aside, she ran her hand over the bedspread.

"Amy," she whispered, tearfully. Letting the net drop back, she turned and came back to me.

"It's all so beautiful. Thank you."

Cradling her head gently in my hands, I tilted her face toward mine. She lifted her lashes to look at me.

"I keep telling you, Lottie. You deserve all the good things."

Bending, I kissed her tremulous lips as they quivered gently under mine. I softened our kiss, sensing that she was feeling overwhelmed.

"Are you hungry?" I asked.

She shook her head. "Not for food. Just for you," she breathed, while pulling my shirt over my head.

Dropping it to the ground, she ran her hands over my chest, making her way to the button on my shorts.

Taking hold of her hands, I stopped her, shaking my head.

"Not yet. We have all night and I want this to last. If you take my shorts off now, it'll be over before it's even begun."

With this, I picked her up and gently placed her on the bed.

I pulled off her sandals and dropped them on the floor, then I started kissing her body, working my way up her legs. She gave a slight shiver as I got to the band of her shorts. After pulling them and her panties off, I breathed in her scent, my mouth watering.

Dropping a kiss to her centre, I made my way up her squirming body, pushing at her shirt until I reached her breasts. Then I pushed the shirt up and, as she raised her arms, I pulled it off her body. Laid out in front of me I took a moment to drink in all that was Lottie. Running my hands back down, I cupped her breasts, stroking her nipples and making her whimper in need. Then I removed her lace-cupped bra so I could get my bare hand on her naked skin.

"Kyle," she breathed, shifting restlessly.

I left nibbling kisses along her neck until I reached her mouth, then planted a long, deep, wet kiss. My cock was so hard it was digging into her as I ground down on her pussy. Pulling away from her mouth, I worked my way back down her body until I got to her breasts again.

Pushing them together, I pulled one nipple into my mouth and sucked. When that one was beautifully hard, I moved to the other and gave it the same treatment. I alternated between sucking on them and then blowing on them gently, always keeping her wanting more.

Lottie was moaning and shifting, her hips rising and falling almost beyond her control.

Her breath hitched and, in a voice filled with need, she murmured, "Kyle, please… I need…"

"What do you need, Angel?"

"You. Just you," she begged.

My cock was so hard that it was painful pushing up against my zipper. Knowing that I had teased both of us enough, I made my way down her body until I got to her legs. Pushing them apart, and wide enough to fit my shoulders between, I took in her pink pussy, wet and glistening. The evidence of her need was slick on her thighs.

Lowering my head, I breathed in her scent, then gave her a long lick from bottom to top, her hips coming off the bed as she wailed and cried out. Gripping her hips, I continued to lick and suck at her clit, then added a finger into her tight pussy. I groaned aloud as I felt how tight she was and knew I'd need to make her come at least once before attempting to have my cock fit in her. As soon as I felt her pussy start to flutter around my finger, I added another and bit down gently on her clit.

Lottie screamed as she came, and the feeling of her clamping down on my fingers while she did, nearly made me lose it. I gently pulled my fingers out of her, then put them to my mouth, groaning as I licked her essence off them. She was shuddering on the bed, her body beautifully flushed from her orgasm. Winding her legs around me, she pulled me towards her.

"Shorts off. NOW!" she demanded.

I hurriedly removed them and tossed them to the side, then moved between her legs. I grabbed hold of my cock and positioned myself at her opening. Her eyelashes fluttered as I rubbed the head of my cock on her clit, her hips rising and falling as I thrust gently against her. Soon I couldn't take anymore and was near bursting. I pushed slowly into her and didn't stop until I felt myself bottom out. Her eyes rolled back in her head. I stilled, waiting for her to adjust to my size. As soon as she relaxed, I started moving, thrusting into her, gently at first until her hips were rising to meet mine with each plunge. I wanted to come but I wouldn't, not until she came one more time.

Looking down, I saw how flushed her gorgeous face was from when she'd come. When I felt her inner walls start to flutter, I knew she was close.

"Angel, I need to see your eyes when you come," I demanded.

She lifted her heavy lids and looked at me under her lashes. The green of her eyes glowing before her eyelids fluttered back down and closed, her lips full and puffy in a slight pout.

With the palm of my hand, I tapped her firmly on the outside of her thigh, her eyes snapped to mine just as her pussy clamped down hard on my cock. I came so hard that for a moment I saw nothing but blackness.

Lowering myself, I caged her in my arms while I caught my breath. I felt her arms go around my back and gently rub up and down in a relaxed way, her legs tightening around my waist.

I pressed my face into her neck, taking deep breaths. Her pulse was beating frantically in her throat, and there was a fine sheen of sweat covering both of us.

I felt her breathing deepen and realised she had fallen asleep. This made me chuckle softly. Gently moving away, I cleaned her up before climbing back into bed and pulling her into my arms.

We woke several times that night, turning to each other. We couldn't get enough of one another's bodies. It seemed that we were making up for the three weeks of not being able to fully bond. In between making love, we ate the dinner that we'd brought. Eventually, we were so tired that we slept, waking up in the early morning. It had started to get cooler, so we got into the hot springs to warm up and soothe our sore muscles.

It was a night that I would never forget. I made up my mind that we would do this as often as possible. Spend time together, just the two of us.

CHAPTER 16

LOTTIE

I woke up early feeling relaxed and well-loved, if a bit stiff, from our activities last night. While I hadn't enjoyed waiting for three weeks, I was glad we had, because we'd got to know each other as a couple before we'd mated, and I think it made our mating sweeter.

I pulled the bedspread up higher in the cool morning breeze. Kyle was still sleeping next to me, his face relaxed and, for once, stress-free in sleep. His lashes cast shadows on his cheeks. Looking towards the table where we'd eaten last night, I saw that someone had dropped off a thermos, and what looked like breakfast.

I quietly slipped out of bed, careful not to wake Kyle, and went to the bag of spare clothes. I put on a pair of sweatpants and a hoodie that must have been Kyle's because it was huge on me. The cool box from last night was gone.

On the table was a note held down by the thermos of coffee. Reading it, I smiled.

Lottie & Kyle,

I thought you would need coffee after last night and I made you some breakfast rolls.

I didn't look, I promise!

Love

Julie

xxx

"That girl." I laughed to myself.

Pouring a cup of coffee and walked over to the hot springs. Before sitting down, I checked for snakes. Not seeing any, I sat on a flat rock and dipped my feet into the water. Sitting there, I heard the sound of the bush waking up. The birds were starting to sing, and in the distance, a troop of monkeys chattered to each other while I sipped my coffee. I loved my home, and mornings like this made me never want to live anywhere else.

Kyle came up behind and sat down with his legs on either side of me. Wrapping his arms tightly around me, he kissed my head, then tucked his face into the side of my neck. At that moment I could say that my life was perfect.

"Morning, Angel," he mumbled, his voice still thick with sleep.

I offered him my coffee, then tipped my head back for a kiss, which he obliged me with.

"Morning, honey," I replied. Leaning back against my mate, I returned my gaze to the springs and that was how we sat sharing a coffee in comfortable silence. Eventually, Kyle sighed. I turned to look at him.

"We have to go," he complained, with a slight pout that made me laugh.

"I know," I agreed. "We can come back here anytime though. And I am looking forward to seeing the others."

"Fine," he groused at me. Getting up, he offered me his hand and pulled me up into his arms. Before I knew it, his mouth was on mine, and I felt his kiss down to my toes. His hands were on my waist, and I felt him push my sweatpants down. Our mouths still joined, I wriggled my hips until my sweatpants fell and I could push them off with my feet. His mouth left mine so he could lift the sweatshirt up and over my head leaving me bare in the morning sun.

Dropping to his knees, he lifted one of my legs over his shoulder then buried his face in my pussy. I lost all coherent thought as he used his tongue and fingers to make me come. My fingers were entangled in his hair as I held on to him and enjoyed the ride. My orgasm hit me slow and easy and just when I thought my legs couldn't hold me for much longer, he lifted me, his hands firm under my arse as I wound my legs around his waist.

I wasn't sure when he'd pushed his shorts out of the way, but he must have because I felt him nudging at my entrance. I let out a sigh as he filled me, and buried my head in his neck, leaving kisses and small bites along the tendons there.

Turning, he moved us back towards the bed, his mouth never leaving mine even as he lowered me down. When he lifted his mouth from mine, and I looked up into his slumberous eyes, I still felt surprised that I had found a male as beautiful as this one, not only in looks but in the way he took care of me and his family.

Through slitted eyes I watched as his body moved above mine. He rocked us gently, never letting go of my gaze. I felt myself getting ready to come again. I knew he was holding back. He moved slightly, and I felt his hand on my clit rubbing in circles, his loving eyes never leaving mine, his were soft and filled with love. My orgasm built slowly, then finally washed over me, leaving behind a warm glow of contentment and satisfaction. Kyle pumped his cock into me faster and faster, coming with a roar.

When he was done, he collapsed over me, breathing deeply as we both came down from our high. He softened and moved to lie next to me on the bed. Both of us were breathing heavily.

"You are going to kill me, woman," he grinned, his eyes alight with laughter.

"ME? I didn't start that round. I was innocently drinking my coffee enjoying the morning," I replied, poking his arm and smiling. I rolled towards him and felt his arm come around my back, pulling me closer until he could drop a kiss on my head.

Sadly, I knew that soon we'd have to get up and head off for the meeting, but for now, it was good to just lie there with my mate, enjoying the afterglow of our time together.

I had a feeling we were going to be late for the meeting but couldn't find it in me to care.

CHAPTER 17

KYLE

After packing up what we could carry on the quad bike and trailer, we finally pulled ourselves away from our haven at the hot springs and headed back to the farm. I'd come back later with Rory and Sean to collect the bed and mattress.

I knew we'd be late getting to the meeting but, what the hell, they could start without us if they needed to.

We were just heading out the door, after getting showered and changed, when I saw Julie lying on the couch with her e-reader, snacks and a drink on the table next to her.

"Are you not going to the meeting with us?" I asked.

She shook her head. "Nope, I decided it was better for me to stay here just in case. Besides, I have snacks and I've just started *Saving Harmony* by Cloe Rowe. I'm set for the day."

"As long as you're sure," Lottie said, concerned at leaving Julie by herself.

"I'm good. I'll meet everyone the next time you all get together. Hopefully, my family will have stopped looking for me by then," she reassured Lottie.

Assured that she was fine, I dropped a kiss on Julie's head and left her to her book. I knew she would be safe as we had upped security around the property since we had been hit by poachers. I wished Lottie and I could stay home as well, but I knew she was looking forward to seeing everyone.

Opening the door to the Land Rover and helping her in, I leaned in to give her a kiss. Running my hands over her shaved hair and cupping her cheeks, I deepened the kiss until we were both breathing hard.

I dropped my head on her shoulder and heaved a sigh, making her laugh.

"Come on, let's go so we can hurry back," she hummed at me, a smile in her voice.

"You'd think they'd have given us at least a week before we had this meeting," I grumbled, getting into the vehicle. I started it up and we were on our way.

Lottie slid from the passenger seat to sit alongside me, her hand on my thigh and her head on my shoulder.

'Thank fuck for bench seats and not having to wear seat belts on back roads,' I thought as she snuggled up to me.

"There, is that better?" she asked, her green eyes sparkling.

"It will do for now," I muttered. "But as soon as this meeting is finished, your arse is in the car and we're coming home."

She gave me a little salute, grinning at me. "Sir! Yes, sir! I will get my behind in the car as soon as lunch is over, Sir!"

"We're staying for lunch?" I groaned, adjusting myself. It was going to be a long day.

She nodded. "We always have lunch, but I'm sure they won't mind if we miss it."

I thought about suggesting we did miss it, but I knew she was looking forward to seeing her sisters and all the other families. They were a tight-knit group and I knew I couldn't do that to her.

Sighing, I said, "Ignore me, Angel. I'm being selfish. We'll stay as long as you want so you can catch up with everyone. Besides, I think your sisters would probably kick my arse if I took you away from them too soon."

That got me a sweet kiss on the cheek. I'd suck it up and spend time with the others so that she could visit them all. It wasn't such a hardship really. Now that she was back to full strength, there was nothing stopping her from travelling to the other farms and ranches. But it seemed my Angel was a bit of a homebody and didn't like to leave the farm unless it was needed. I was happy with that because it meant I had less to worry about and I would be with her if we had to go anywhere.

We travelled silently for the next hour, content in each other's company. Lottie gave me directions when we got closer to the turn-off for the meeting. Up ahead, I saw other vehicles had already turned up, and everyone was milling around outside, obviously waiting for us to arrive.

Lottie sat up straight and I could see the excitement in her face.

As I stopped the vehicle, she started to get out. I stopped her with a hand on her thigh.

"Angel, wait. I'll come around and help you," I said.

She rolled her eyes at me. "I'm not hurt anymore, Kyle."

"I know, Angel, but just humour me, okay? For now, I need to do this."

She gave me a tender look, her eyes soft. "Okay, honey, but hurry, I can't wait to see everyone."

Getting out and rounding the vehicle, I helped her out, pressing a quick kiss to her mouth as she slid down my body, making me groan. The door was hiding our bodies so I took the opportunity to adjust myself. Lottie's eyes dropped to my hand, then lifted to mine. I saw hers were heated.

"Hurry up, you two," I heard her sister Ava shout.

Lottie groaned, her head hitting my shoulder. "I'm so on board with you, honey. Do the meeting, a fast lunch, and home as quickly as possible. And I may have to kill my sister before then."

I laughed at her. Closing the door, I put my arm around her shoulders and we walked to the others. Her sisters were shifting their feet excitedly like they hadn't just seen her yesterday.

"Kyle!" It was my mother's voice. With a sigh, I let Lottie out from under my arm as she was surrounded by the other females. As I passed them, I dropped a kiss on my mother's cheek before I moved on to greet the males.

My brothers were grinning at me. "How did Lottie like what you had organised for her?"

I smirked. "What do you think? I can definitely recommend the hot springs if you want to spend a romantic night in the open."

Rory and Sean laughed.

"All Amy would talk about last night was how romantic you were and how lucky Lottie was. I tell you, brother, I'm not sure if we're going to be able to top it. We've been struggling to think of what we can do for her. Our mating happened so quickly and, with everything that's been happening, we haven't had a chance to really make her feel special," Sean said.

"What are you guys talking about?" asked Anton, who'd just walked over.

Sean told Anton and the other males what I'd done to make Lottie's evening special.

I saw them looking at me with surprise. "Jesus, we know who to come to for romance advice when we eventually find mates," joked Luca.

I shrugged. I didn't think it was that much of a big deal, I just wanted her to know that she'd always come first for me, and I'd do whatever it took to make sure she always knew that. Lottie hadn't ever been put first in anything and had been overlooked and badly treated by the main male in her life. I wanted her to know I'd never treat her that way.

When I explained it, they all seemed surprised, except for Dex, and surprisingly, Duke. Both of them nodded.

"Why are you nodding? You don't have a mate," Zane said to Duke.

"Just because I don't have a mate yet doesn't mean I don't watch how other mated couple's act. When I find my mate, I want her to know that she'll always be my top priority. What Kyle said is all true. Our mates should always come first, before anything else and if they don't, then maybe they weren't our proper mate. You'll know when the right one comes along, or your animal will," Duke said.

Finally, the females were done greeting Lottie and came over to us. I thought I might get my Angel back but, no, the other males in her life had to welcome her back first, including my idiot brothers. Like they didn't see her every day. I knew they were doing it to mess with me.

After she had been passed around and hugged by all, I'd had enough and almost pulled her away from Joel who was the last to hug her. The others had all gone into the meeting room and it was only Joel and Amy left outside with us. As I put my arm around Lottie's waist, Joel stopped me with his question.

"What's that smell?" he asked, sniffing at her neck and causing my gorilla to start rumbling in my chest. I could feel my face start to change.

Amy moved up next to her brother and put her hand on his chest to move him away from Lottie. "Joel, you need to move back and stop sniffing Lottie before Kyle decides to tear you apart for sniffing his mate."

Ignoring her, he sniffed and then pushed his face into Amy's shoulder. "You smell the same but not as much. Cinnamon and sugar," he muttered. "Annie smells the same." He shook himself and pulled back.

I could see he was confused and his eyes were glowing with his animal.

"Sorry, Kyle. Not sure what it is, but the smell is driving my animal nuts. It's not the females. It's something on their clothing." He shrugged. "Guess I'll stay away from them for now. Maybe it's something in your house?"

Turning away, he went into the meeting room. Lottie, Amy and I stood looking at each other. We all discreetly sniffed ourselves and each other but couldn't smell anything unusual.

"I think my brother's losing it. Must be the strain of running the farm by himself," Amy sniggered, heading into the meeting room with us close behind.

Pulling out a chair, I sat down, pulling Lottie down onto my lap. I saw the other mated pair doing the same. Clearly, we all needed to feel our mates close.

Dex called the meeting to order. First of all, he explained the recent changes, including the bartering system that we had already covered with Amy and Lottie. Dex also talked about Mum opening a shop in town so she could sell her jams and sauces exclusively through it. The MacGregors had a shop that was sitting empty, waiting to be filled. I knew Mum was interested, but I also knew she'd want to speak to us before she agreed to anything. It was how our family worked. Dex and Mum decided they'd each put forward a proposal and then discuss it at the next meeting.

Business over, we went and unpacked the food and set-up tables and chairs in the shade of the trees.

I enjoyed spending time with the families, and it was easy to see the benefits of us joining them, not just financially, but also for support and protection.

CHAPTER 18

LOTTIE

I loved seeing everyone at the meeting. Reggie was sporting a little baby bump. I watched her and Dex together and you could see the love in every glance. It made me wonder if that was how Kyle and I looked at each other.

My sisters wanted to know how our night at the hot springs had gone, so I told them what Kyle had done with the help of his brothers, Amy, and Julie. Amy made it clear that it was all Kyle's idea, all they had done was help implement it.

Marie sighed, looking at my mate. "That's so romantic. I hope I find a good one like you have, Lottie. If not, I'm hiring Kyle to give him lessons," she stated, making us all laugh.

Going over to the males, I was grabbed and hugged by them all, including his brothers who decided to mess with him, making Kyle's gorilla rumble in his chest. There was a lot of laughter and teasing. Joel was the last one to hug me as the others drifted into the meeting room.

I was taken by surprise when he started to sniff me. This wasn't like Joel at all, he was always so reserved. I wondered what was up with him. He kept muttering something about, *'Cinnamon and sugar.'*

Eventually when I thought Kyle was going to lose it, Amy stepped forward and gently pushed Joel away, only to get the same sniffing treatment. We were confused. Joel eventually pulled himself together and apologised before we joined the others in the meeting room.

Once the meeting was done, we all went outside to set up tables and chairs and get the food out of the vehicles. We sat outside in the shade of the huge trees, chatting and catching up on the non-business side of our lives. All the families were now aware of Julie's situation and that they should be wary of strangers asking questions about her. Kyle explained that she hadn't come today, because she didn't feel safe to do so. This didn't go down well with the families. I knew that, if need be, Julie would be moved between the families until her biological family was dealt with.

We had all barely settled down when Renee asked the question I'd been dreading, but that also desperately needed answering.

"Annie, will you tell us about our family and why our father hates Lottie so much?"

Annie sighed, looking at me with soft eyes. "I will, Renee, but not today."

I breathed a sigh of relief. Kyle pulled me tighter into his arms, pressing a kiss to my head.

"Why not today?" asked Dex.

"I'm still waiting for confirmation on some of the information before I tell anyone. I also wanted to check with Lottie to see if she was happy with me telling everyone or if she just wanted her sisters to know." She looked at me carefully, her face filled with concern.

I felt a chill go over my body at her look, and goosebumps rose on my skin. Kyle held me closer and ran his hands over my arms to warm me.

Sighing, I looked around at the familiar faces of those that I called my family, stopping at Renee. I saw the concern on her face.

"Whatever you want to do, Lottie, we'll all be here for you, no matter what," she declared.

Renee's words made my mind up. Turning back to Annie, I said, "I think we all need to hear what the reason is, Annie. I'd like to know as soon as possible though, please. I just want to put it all behind me and enjoy the rest of my life without this secret hanging over my head."

Annie nodded, her face soft as she reached for my hand and held on tight. "I should be hearing back soon regarding the last piece of the information. As soon as I know, we can arrange to get together. Until then, don't worry. Enjoy your time with Kyle and concentrate on getting your business set up, okay?"

I nodded, tears filling my eyes. I figured if I'd lived without knowing why my father had hated me all my life, a few more weeks wouldn't make a difference.

With that, we started packing up, getting ready to go our separate ways. I noticed that Joel was still looking unsettled, and saw Amy, Sean and Rory speaking to him.

Amy asked me if we could take Annie back with us as they were going to spend the night with Joel. I could see she was concerned about her brother.

Kyle helped Annie and me into his Land Rover before going across to speak to his brothers, reassuring them that he could handle anything that came up.

We watched them drive away, Joel following on his motorbike.

As I watched them leave, I said to Annie, "I hope Joel's okay. I've never seen him so unsettled. He's usually so quiet and solid."

Annie just smiled serenely, as if she knew something that I didn't, and patted my leg. "Joel is going to be just fine, Lottie. Don't you worry."

At this comment, Kyle looked at me with raised eyebrows. I just shrugged. I figured Annie would share when she was ready.

Driving away, my eyes closed drowsily as we drove back home. I fell asleep with my head on Kyle's shoulder, his hand holding firm on my leg. I felt a deep contentment.

CHAPTER 19

KYLE

The next few weeks were spent getting our businesses going, partly so we'd have something to talk about during the family meetings. Contracts were signed for the shop that Mum and Dex had opened in town, selling her jams and sauces. She also included examples of my leather work and Rory's furniture. Amy came to her with a stock of quilts and bedspreads, and these were added to inventory on the basis of when they were gone, they were gone. Customer orders wouldn't be taken, as Amy didn't have the time and could only add stock as and when she was able to replete her inventory.

The shop was so well received my mum put the word out that they'd stock art and handmade crafts from other suppliers for a small commission.

We needed someone to manage the store and ended up employing John, our former pilot, since he was really bored being retired. He'd run his flying business for over thirty years, so knew how to manage a business and was great at dealing with people. Everyone was happy with the decision, especially John's wife. Having him home all the time was driving her mad and, according to the local grapevine, she was about ready to murder him.

Lottie was back to training horses and was starting to take on new clients. Mum and I went to see the set up at the Moore farm and took notes. Lottie definitely needed more than we'd planned for but we got to it. We were busy building an undercover training ring, as well as adding to the stables and building a bigger tack room.

Amy joined us for a meeting with Lottie, since she was the family accountant for the Landrys and the Moores. Zane MacGregor did the family accounts for the Russos and MacGregors, but both worked on the accounts for the various businesses that the four families owned together. Amy added us to their workload. She was talking about bringing in Ava and Marie to help, once they were done with college, because Zane and her were struggling to keep up with the growing businesses.

Our lives had changed so much in such a short time. It made it hard to spend time together, just Lottie and me. We seemed to only see each other alone in the evening and the early morning. Mealtimes were mostly family affairs.

I made sure Lottie knew she was my number one priority as much as possible, and we soon settled into a smooth rhythm. One afternoon, Mum let me know that she'd heard back from her source about the last bit of information regarding Lottie's family. She planned to talk to Lottie first, then set up a meeting with the others since Lottie felt we'd all been through so much together that they deserved to be there when she found out the truth.

We were all sitting down at supper, talking about our day when Mum caught my eye. I covered Lottie's hand with mine and threaded my fingers through hers. She looked at me startled, but then gave me her sunny smile. I hated that this was going to make her lose the happiness that was showing on it.

Mum cleared her throat and we all turned to look at her. She gave Lottie an encouraging smile. "Lottie, I have the last bit of information I was waiting for. You just need to let me know when, or if, you would like me to tell the others."

Lottie went pale and, with a trembling hand, she reached for her glass of water. She took a sip then, setting the glass down, she nervously rubbed a hand down her shorts before looking at me.

I brought her hand up to my lips and kissed it. "Whatever you want, Lottie. You don't have to do this if you don't want to. You don't ever have to see him again. From the moment he hit you, he forfeited the right to have anything to do with you."

Lottie smiled shakily at me, her eyes filling with tears. She blinked rapidly, trying to stop them from spilling. "I know, honey, but I have to know, and even if I didn't, my sisters do. It won't be so bad with you there."

Turning to my mum, I said, "Can we set it up for as soon as possible? I don't want to wait and have this hanging over us any longer. Where would be the best place?"

Amy answered. "I know you probably don't want to go back there anytime soon, Lottie, but The Lake seems the best place for us all to meet. If you want, I can call Luca and see when it's free next?"

Lottie nodded. "Good idea, Amy. I don't want what happened there to spoil it for me. I love The Lake. Let's start afresh where it all began for Kyle and me. I like that idea."

Amy got up and left the table, picking up her phone as she went. The rest of us stayed and made small talk while we waited for her to come back. I was glad Mum had waited until after we had eaten, as I could see Lottie was struggling.

About twenty minutes later, Amy returned. Going to Lottie, she pulled her out of her chair for a hug. "I've spoken to all the families, and Luca has booked us in for Friday through to Sunday. They'll all be there despite the short notice. We decided that no matter what Annie has to tell us, it's always been our special place to relax, and we're going to do that no matter what. You're very important to us, Lottie, and we all love you. Whatever the deal is with your father, that won't change, ever."

Releasing Lottie, Amy looked at her childhood friend and smiled, wiping at the tears that were running down Lottie's face. Lottie hugged Amy close.

"Thank you, Amy. I don't know what I'd do without you sometimes."

Amy shrugged. "You're my family. How often did I hide at your family's place to get away from the craziness that was my family? Could you come with me for a minute? I have something for you."

I loved how my brothers' mate was with Lottie. I knew they had grown up together, and it seemed that the two of them had always been close.

Amy turned to the rest of us and said firmly, "Don't any of you leave. Lottie and I will be back shortly," she declared, before pulling Lottie with her to the back door.

CHAPTER 20

LOTTIE

After hearing the news from Annie, my stomach was churning. I'd known it would be coming soon, but I'd done a good job of ignoring it over the last couple of weeks.

Now, I was being tugged out the door by Amy. It seemed there was something she had to show me. I wondered what it was, and why tonight? All I wanted to do was curl up in bed with Kyle and sleep the next couple of days away, so we could get to the weekend and get it over and done with.

Amy stopped at the foot of the garden and I looked around for what she wanted to show me.

Taking a breath, she looked at me, her eyes large and her head tilted to one side. She was biting her lip nervously, so I shook the hand I was still holding. "What's up Amy? Just tell me. You look like you're about to pass out."

"Okay, I'm not sure how you're going to feel about it. I do know if it was me, I wouldn't be happy about it so early in my mating."

"Amy, just spit it out. What wouldn't you be happy about?"

"You're pregnant. Not far along from the scent of you. I noticed it when I hugged you this evening. The others probably can't scent it yet, as their noses aren't as sensitive as mine."

I closed my eyes and rested my hands over my stomach where Kyle and my baby was and felt nothing but peace and happiness. A wide smile broke over my face as I looked at my long-time friend who was waiting anxiously for me to say something.

Seeing my look of delight, her own face broke out in a smile of relief. "You're happy," she breathed.

"So happy, Amy. It's just what I needed to hear tonight. Why did you think I wouldn't be happy?"

"You haven't been mated very long, and I was worried that you'd think it was too soon. You know how I grew up, Lottie. I haven't said anything to Rory and Sean, but I'm dreading going into heat. The thought of being with pup fills me with dread."

I enclosed my friend in my arms. "Oh, Amy. You need to speak to your mates before then. Being pregnant is a gift. Speak to them. You shouldn't worry, we'll all be here to help. It won't be like with your parents."

She nodded and looked at me sadly. "Logically, I know that, but I'm still terrified. Luckily, I have a few months still to worry about that. Are you going to tell everyone tonight?"

I nodded. "Yeah, I think we all need some good news. Does your nose have an idea of how many weeks along I am?"

Amy laughed, linking her arm with mine as we walked to the main house. "About two weeks."

Back in the house, the family was still sitting around the table, chatting and waiting for us to come back.

Kyle was watching for me, and his eyes warmed when we came through the back door. Amy left my side to go back to Sean and Rory. I went over to Kyle and pressed a kiss to his cheek. Cupping his face in my hands, I looked into his blue eyes. He looked concerned. He took my wrists in his hands as his eyes searched mine.

"What's wrong, Angel?"

"Nothing, honey. Everything is good with me and hopefully will be good with you."

He looked puzzled. "Okay?" he said, turning the word into a question.

Releasing him, I turned to the table. Everyone was watching me.

"In approximately eight and half months, Kyle will be a daddy." I grinned so hard my face hurt.

For a few seconds, the silence was deafening, but then they all started cheering. Annie started crying. And Kyle, my gorgeous Kyle, sat there stunned as he took in my announcement.

Then his face lit with a smile, the happiness radiating out from him. Grabbing me gently, he kissed me soft and slow, holding me tight in his arms. He buried his face in my neck, and his shoulders began to shake. I held on tight as our emotions got the better of us. Everyone was eager to congratulate us, but I did notice Sean and Rory giving Amy looks. I hoped she would talk to them soon about her concerns.

Julie was beyond excited, making all kinds of plans and the baby wasn't even here yet. Although Annie had tears in her eyes, she didn't seem that excited. She was smiling, but there was a reserve about her that seemed unusual.

Kyle was ready to call Jett and have him come and check on me, but Julie laughingly told him that there was nothing for Jett to do except confirm the pregnancy and if Amy had already smelt it, we didn't need any medical confirmation.

I was looking forward to telling my sisters, but that could wait until the weekend.

Once all the excitement had died down, Kyle picked me up bridal-style and took me to bed. Laying me down gently, I looked up at him. His eyes were so soft and full of love.

"I love you, Lottie. I don't know what I did to deserve you, but I'm so happy that I met you that night. Thank you for this wonderful gift," he said, putting his hands tenderly on my stomach.

Reaching up, I kissed him, a kiss so long and deep I felt it to the bottom of my soul. I grabbed the bottom of his shirt and pulled it up so I could get my hands on his skin. He pulled it over his head and dropped it to the floor, while I was hooking my toes in the band of his shorts and pushing them down. His hands pushed up my skirt and gripped my hips. Undoing the bows at the top of my shoulders, my dress fell open, leaving me covered only by my strapless bra, with the tops of my breasts pushing up against it. Kyle then made his way down my neck, leaving a trail of wet kisses. When he reached the tops of my breasts, he undid the front clasp and they sprang free from the delicate fabric. Immediately, he bit down on one nipple, making me whimper with desire.

It felt so good. I could feel the slickness of my need soaking through my panties and coating my thighs. Leaving my breasts, Kyle went down my body, kissing and biting gently until he came to the small rise of my belly, which he showered with gentle kisses. Moving down, he reached my pussy and hooked his fingers into the sides of my panties. He ripped them from me and I gave an involuntary gasp. Bringing them to his face, he took a deep breath, inhaling the smell of my arousal. His gorilla showed, and his teeth elongated slightly as he looked at me through hooded eyes.

Running his fingers through my juices, he gently inserted his fingers into me and scissored them. My hips rose and I watched as he brought his fingers to his mouth, sucking my juices from them. He pushed his legs tight up against me, his legs cushioning my hips. His cock looked painfully hard standing up against his belly.

Gently he pushed into me, his eyes closing as his face tightened. He pulled me up against him until he could reach my mouth. Holding me tight against his front, his chest hard against my breasts,

I rubbed against him as he rocked into me, hitting my clit just right. My arms were around his shoulders as I buried my head into the crook of his neck. I felt his mouth on my shoulder, gently biting down with each thrust of his hips. Just as I was about to come, he bit down hard, marking me as his. It was the first time his gorilla had done this during sex, and it make me clench down hard on his cock. Then I came, and kept coming as he gripped my hips, pulling me hard against him. With a moan, he came, and his cock pulsed deep within me.

As we came down, he lay kisses gently along my shoulder and neck, then feathered them across my cheeks and my eyelids until he came to my mouth. Kissing me long and deep, he slowly softened and slipped out of me. My eyes started closing drowsily as he lay me down gently.

He cleaned us both up, then pulled the covers over us. We spooned, and he held onto me tightly, one hand protectively covering my belly as we drifted off, content.

CHAPTER 21

KYLE

I woke early the next morning, Lottie still asleep in my arms, her face peaceful in the early morning light coming through the windows and my hand still protectively cupping her flat belly. I couldn't wait for her to grow big and round with our child.

We'd slept later than normal and the rest of the house was stirring. Dropping a gentle kiss on Lottie's head, I eased out of bed, careful not to wake her. I knew today was going to be an emotional day for her. My mother had given me the bare bones of the story, so I knew more or less what to expect. Quietly getting showered and dressed, I made my way out to the others in the kitchen. Amy and Julie turned as I came in.

"Where's Lottie?" asked Amy.

"I left her sleeping. I figured with the amount of emotional stress today is going to put on her, I'd let her sleep as long as possible."

Julie nodded in agreement, then kissed my cheek as she handed me my coffee. Patting my shoulder, she said, "You're a good mate, Kyle."

I shrugged at this. I didn't think looking after your mate was something that should be hard. I wanted Lottie to be happy, because if she was happy then I felt like I'd done my job well.

Over breakfast, we talked about what to take to the Lake. Amy said not to worry about anything, but just to pack clothing for Lottie and me. As Lottie still hadn't woken up, Julie prepared a tray for her, handing it to me as I left the kitchen.

Entering the bedroom, I found her still asleep, her face untroubled. I hoped that I could keep it that way. Putting the tray down on the bedside table, I wondered how she'd take not being able to have her morning coffee. From what I understood, Dex's mate Reggie had not been happy when she found out.

Laying on the bed next to her, I ran my finger gently down her face from her temple to her chin until she started to wake. Dropping a soft kiss on her soft, plump, lips, I watched as her eyes slowly opened, still hazy with sleep.

She smiled up at me. "Morning, handsome."

I couldn't resist that mouth. Leaning in, I ran my tongue over her bottom lip and nipped at it slightly. Her mouth opened for mine and I deepened the kiss. Her arms came around me as she moved onto her back, taking me with her. We got lost in each other until we heard a knock on the door. Lottie giggled into my neck, which made me feel less murderous to the person doing the knocking.

"Kyle? We're leaving," shouted Rory through the door. "We have everything, just bring yourselves. Julie is staying here, as a couple of people have turned up at the clinic. Check on her before you leave, please."

I rolled my eyes. As if we wouldn't check on her anyway.

"Thanks, Rory," Lottie shouted, her voice full of laughter.

"Morning, beautiful!" he shouted back through the door. I picked up my boot and threw it at the door. Rory gave a bark of laughter as he moved away.

Turning back to the bed, I found Lottie leaning back against the headboard drinking her orange juice. I couldn't believe that this gorgeous female was mine. Her hair was slowly growing back and had a slight curl to it. Her green eyes sparkled with happiness as she looked at me. The sheet was tucked tight under her arms hiding her beautiful breasts.

Sighing, I sat back down on the bed and put the breakfast tray on her lap. "Eat, Angel. I'll pack while you do. Just tell me what you want to take."

Grabbing a backpack from the wardrobe, I packed clothes for myself, then followed instructions from Lottie on what she wanted. When it came to her swimming costume, I held up two scraps of black material that didn't seem to have much coverage.

"Angel, don't you have another one somewhere?" I grunted, holding the scraps up by my fingertips in disgust.

Lottie laughed. "Honey, I always wear that bikini. Everyone's seen me in it. None of them see me the way you do. Don't forget, we grew up together, so they saw it all when we used to skinny dip as kids," she chuckled.

I growled at her, feeling like my head was going to explode just knowing that other males had seen what was mine. Lottie continued to be amused. She got out of bed and sauntered naked over to where I was standing by the dresser.

Hands on my chest, she looked up at me, her eyes bright with amusement. "We were kids, honey, but just to make you feel better, think about your brothers and Amy. She grew up with us too, remember, and used to skinny dip as well. In fact, I think there was also kissing involved, just so you know." She grinned at me, patted my chest, and laughed her way to the bathroom.

A smile lit up my face as I thought of how I could now torture my brothers. With this thought, I followed my angel into the shower.

CHAPTER 22

LOTTIE

My morning had been filled with laughter and, surprisingly, I wasn't worried or concerned about what Annie had to tell us. I just wanted it over so I could enjoy my pregnancy, my mate, and my new family.

We checked on Julie before leaving, and she was as busy as anything at the clinic. There seemed to have been a chickenpox outbreak in the village, so she was handing out calamine lotion and paracetamol to concerned mothers. There were also the usual cases of injuries that needed stitches, which were a daily occurrence. Apparently, people used to stitch themselves before Julie came.

The foreman had assured us that he would be on the radio if he needed us to come back early. We reminded him that he should look out for strangers and not allow anyone up to the house. A security gate had been built on the road up to the house and this had a guard on it twenty-four hours a day.

We were in Kyle's Land Rover. It was a Series II short wheelbase. A classic from the 1970s, his father had left it to him, and he had rebuilt it from scratch. It was his baby. I didn't mind traveling in it as the bench seat always allowed me to cuddle up next to him.

"Honey, they were ten when she kissed them," I laughed, as we bounced along on our journey to The Lake.

"Doesn't matter. I can still torture my brothers. It's what we do," he replied.

"Hmm, just remember that Anton and Luca will be dragged into it and I don't need them hating you," I advised.

"They won't," he assured me. "I sent them a message before we left, as there's no signal at The Lake. They are totally up for torturing Rory and Sean," he said, grinning.

I shook my head, hoping that nobody would need stitches at the end of the day. I wasn't too worried though because Jett would be there, so it shouldn't be too bad, and Annie wouldn't let it get out of hand. I did need to give Amy a heads-up though.

We were the last to arrive, which seemed to be the way it was since Kyle and I got mated. Kyle grabbed our bags from the back and we walked up to the rondavel and fire pit where the others were gathered.

Most of them were already in swimming costumes and I saw the boats were already in the water. I guess Annie was in no hurry to tell us my family story.

My sisters were the first to see us coming and ran over to say hello. Kyle grudgingly relinquished me to them, making it into a big deal with Ava and Marie. They always fell into his trap, not realising he wasn't serious, but it amused Renee and me to no end.

Ava pushed him, not moving him an inch. "Go away, it's sister time. Go and hassle your brothers."

"You know Ava, that's a fantastic idea," he smirked, looking a little evil. He dropped a kiss on my head then went towards his brothers who were standing with Amy between them.

"What was that about?" Renee asked, looking at me.

Shrugging, I cringed a little. "I may have let slip that Amy kissed Anton and Luca years ago. Rory interrupted us this morning, and Kyle sees this as perfect pay back. Anton and Luca are in on it by the way."

Renee, Ava, and Marie looked at me, their mouths open in surprise. "Oh,

Lottie, that might not have been a great idea."

Feeling slightly ashamed, I nodded. "I know. I need to go and warn Amy."

Just then we heard a squeal, and then the distinctive sound of an angry gorilla.

Up ahead, we saw Anton and Luca running with Sean and Rory chasing them. Luckily none had changed into their animals yet, but I could see that it was a close thing with Rory and Sean.

Amy was shouting at them, but they weren't listening "We were kids, you big behemoths! I was TEN!"

We started towards them, not that I was sure what I could do to calm things down. To be fair, nobody else looked that worried and, except for Amy, everybody else seemed amused, including Annie.

Soon Anton and Luca were tiring after running all around the camp to get away from two angry gorillas. Realising that

Annie was their only hope of salvation they ran over and put their arms around her and hung on, laughing so much that her body was shaking from it.

Annie put both her hands up. "Boys, STOP!" she shouted firmly.

This seemed to penetrate the brothers' rage, as they saw their mother meant business.

She spoke to them firmly, "If you two would calm down, you'd see that Kyle is getting back at you for interrupting him and Lottie this morning. I swear, you lot are no better now than when you were toddlers. Amy and these boys were only children when they kissed."

This caused the twins to rumble again, but Annie was adamant.

"Don't you start with me. Think a little, and then go and see to your mate. You've upset her enough for the day, don't you think?" she barked at them.

She turned and pointed a finger at Kyle. "And don't think I'm done with you either. This could have caused major issues for something so small. I swear you and your brothers will drive me to drink."

Spinning around, she drilled a finger into each of Anton and Luca's chests. "And you two, what on earth made you think antagonizing two gorillas would be a good idea. Do you have any idea what they could have done to you if I wasn't here?"

Looking sheepish, Anton and Luca gave her a kiss on either cheek. "Sorry, Annie, we didn't think. We're used to pulling pranks and none of us are used to having mates. We'll apologise to them," Anton assured her.

"Okay." She patted them each on the cheek as if they were her own sons, then walked away to the fire pit.

I thought all was calm after all the males apologised, but then I realised that Amy had been crying which made me feel guilty. She wasn't crying any more though. She was after my blood.

She stomped her way over to me, her eyes spitting fire.

She pointed a finger at me and I braced myself for a tongue lashing. "You! What type of friend are you? You couldn't give me a heads-up first so I was prepared and could have enjoyed it rather than being scared out of my mind. I swear if you weren't pregnant, I would beat your arse," she yelled at me.

I felt a bit sheepish, I pulled her into a hug in apology and I figured she wasn't really too angry with me when she returned the hug.

Then I registered what she had said as I heard my sisters shout in unison, "PREGNANT!"

There was a lot of whooping and hollering from everyone and I was passed around for hugs and kisses of congratulations. Kyle got the same treatment but with added back poundings.

I saw Reggie grinning at me. At nearly three months gone, her belly was the size of a watermelon.

"So, if I recall correctly, about six weeks ago in this same spot, you were declaring that you probably wouldn't mate and would leave that to your sisters. Now look at you, mated and expecting." Gripping my hands tightly, she pulled me in for a hug.

"Are you happy, Lottie?" she whispered.

"So happy, Reggie," I whispered back.

"Good. You deserve all the best things in life," Reggie said.

We let go of each other and wiped the tears away, laughing at each other.

Feeling strong arms surround my waist, I tilted my head back to look at Kyle and was rewarded with a kiss.

It was good seeing the happiness on everyone's faces, and I knew that no matter what Annie had to tell us, we would make it through because of the loving support network that surrounded us.

CHAPTER 23

ANNIE

Considering everything that had gone on today, it had been a good day filled with laughter and family. I hadn't been able to let them know about the Moore family history as quickly as I'd wanted, as Chief Abioye the Sixth had asked me to wait as he wanted to be there when I told them.

We were all sitting around the fire chatting while we waited for him to arrive. I looked at all those I regarded as my children and felt a deep sense of contentment. Lottie was wrapped in a blanket sitting between Kyle's legs, leaning against his chest while she talked to Reggie who was in a similar position with Dex. It was so good to see Kyle so happy. He'd always been my serious boy and I'd worried that he'd never find someone to help him lighten up, but Lottie had done the job. I was anxiously waiting for my first grandchild but I knew it would all be worth it.

Rory, Sean, and Amy were sitting on a bean bag, all snuggled up in a pile. I loved watching the dynamics between those three, although I sensed there may be trouble brewing. I could see how anxious Amy was when Lottie had shared the news of her pregnancy. I think Lottie knew what the problem was, but wouldn't share as she was extremely loyal to Amy. I decided that all I could do was just be there for them.

When the Chief and his entourage appeared out of nowhere, we were all startled.

With him were his personal guards, all armed with traditional shields and spears that denoted them the Chief's Guard. I did notice that each carried a handgun as well, but these were less visible, under their arms in leather holsters. Each guard was dressed in khaki shorts and shirtless, they had obviously decided to run over as their chests were heaving and glistening with sweat.

The Chief, still a handsome man in his early fifties, hadn't lost any of his charisma and was dressed much the same as his guards but was also wearing his ceremonial arm bands on his biceps. His chest was still as broad and muscled as when had been a young man and I knew he still trained with his guards to keep fit, he too was also armed with a handgun.

Along with the Chief was his current witchdoctor, who was not much older than the Chief. He was also in shorts and around his neck was a necklace made of bones and feathers adorned his hair. And while not as large as the men surrounding him, he was still a handsome man. He was currently removing his ceremonial robe from a bag.

Dex took the lead in greeting the Chief, and once all the formalities were done with and refreshments offered, we got as comfortable as we could, considering I was about to tell a story that spanned generations and had caused untold grief to all parties involved.

The Chief looked at me and motioned for me to start the story. I knew he'd interrupt if he felt it necessary. His command of the facts of the story were greater than mine, and in my nervousness, I might forget something important.

Taking a deep breath, I started a story that had started from pieces picked up here and there but had been completed by a visit with the Chief at the main village.

"Okay, I know you're all keen to find out what happened to make Frank the way he is. It's a long story and not a pretty one. Please bear with the Chief and me as we explain."

Around the fire the group grew silent, and I began.

"*It started with Frank's father, Frank Senior. In those days, the four families met at the Chief's palace in the main village to discuss all that was being done and to make the chief aware of any issues or problems that the families were struggling with. The particular meeting I am going to talk about was the same as any other. There was food and drink in abundance and everyone was getting on as well as they usually did. Or so they all thought.*"

"*Nobody had noticed that Frank Senior had disappeared during the meal until screaming and shouting was heard coming from a hut not far from the Chief's.*"

"*Now the Chief had a daughter that he revered above all else, since she was his only daughter. She was extremely beautiful and had been promised to the son of the Chief of another tribe. The hope was that their mating would create peace between the two tribes and put a stop to the strife and violence between them."*

"When people got to the hut, they found a terrible scene inside. Frank Senior was lying unconscious on the ground, naked and covered with blood, beside him was the Chief's daughter. She had been violated in the worst way and her throat had been slit. In Frank Senior's hand was a bloody knife."

"Pandemonium ensued as you can imagine, and Frank Senior was taken into custody. When they finally managed to wake him, he claimed he had no knowledge of what they were talking about. He kept insisting that he'd never do something like that when he had a mate he loved. But the Chief was mad with grief. All thought that he would have Frank killed, but the punishment he had in mind was far crueller."

"Frank Senior's mate was a beautiful human woman called Molly. She was soft and gentle and loved by all on the

farm and by all the families. Molly and Frank already had a son who was five years old. That son was Frank Junior. Molly was also pregnant with Frank's second child."

"The Chief called for the witchdoctor and demanded he curse Frank's bloodline. The witchdoctor advised that the heat of the moment was not a good time to make such decisions, but the Chief was adamant. He wanted it done then and there. From what we understand, the gist of the curse was as follows."

"The Moore line would never have another male born to it. If a male was conceived, it would die at birth. Every child born of the Moore line would be female."

"The witchdoctor did manage to put a caveat in that the curse would be broken once a female child born of that line was able to shift into their animal in the year of their twelfth birthday. Until that happened the curse would continue."

"What followed was truly a tragedy. The four families were sent home unable to believe what had happened. Frank Senior kept saying he was innocent, but the only one who believed him was his mate."

"About two weeks after this happened, Frank Senior's mate Molly, the Moore sisters' grandmother, went into early labour at six months and gave birth to a stillborn boy. Frank Senior slipped into a deep depression and started making plans for his own passing. He updated his will to leave everything to his mate and son, then started to fashion a guillotine in secret. It's not easy for a shifter to commit suicide. We heal so quickly that drastic means are needed."

"The guillotine was designed so that the lever was accessible only to the person who was under it. He wrote letters to the heads of each family and to his mate. Then one night, he did the unthinkable, pulled that lever. In the letters he said that he couldn't believe he'd done the things he was accused of, but if he had *done them then he didn't want the curse to continue with him. He hoped that if he was dead then the curse would be broken."*

"About a week after Frank Senior killed himself, it was found that the whole thing was a set up. The Chief's daughter had been killed by a third tribe that didn't want the first two tribes to become allies with the marriage of the Chief's daughter. They'd needed a scapegoat, and as the four families were partly responsible for the security for the tribe, this was seen as a good way to weaken them."

"They drugged Frank Senior's drink and made it look as if it had been him that had violated and murdered the Chief's daughter. The Chief was horrified at what he had done and had tried to make amends, but as the witchdoctor had warned him, a curse spoken in anger and grief was unbreakable outside of the caveat he had managed to include."

"Frank Junior grew up and was completely different from the man he is now. He was charismatic and happy, very well-liked by the ladies. He thought the curse was over now that his father was dead. His mother tried to tell him that the curse would continue, but he wouldn't listen. I guess he was young and thought himself invincible."

"He met Renee's mother Cara in town and, although they weren't mates, they spent time together and Cara fell pregnant. He had her come out to the farm to live, but she hated it there. As soon as Renee was born, her mother signed all her rights over to Frank Junior and left. Frank Senior's mate Molly was by now in her sixties and struggling a bit to help with childcare, so your father decided to hire a nanny for Renee. He did love you, Renee. I remember the way he was with you. He was an attentive father."

"He found a nanny in Lottie's mother, Sarah. She was around eighteen when Frank took her on. Her father owed

Frank money, and this was his way of paying it back. Free labour in the form of Lottie's mother."

"I don't think either of them expected to become mates, but they did, and Frank Junior was happy, so happy. Seeing the two of them together was beautiful and, when they came into town with Renee, they looked like the perfect family. Within a year, Sarah was expecting and Frank was over the moon. His mother cautioned them, but they thought young love would triumph."

"Sarah's pregnancy showed no problems until she went into labour. She was eight months along when she went into labour and there wasn't time to get her to the hospital. Molly radioed for help as Frank Junior was away at a family meeting and she was by herself with Sarah. I went over to see what I could do. Unbeknown to us, the Chief's guilty conscience meant that he'd kept tabs on the family and sent one of his midwives to help with the birth. Sarah was about three hours into labour when

the midwife and I knew that things weren't right. Molly went to check on you, Renee. When she came back, her words were, 'I told them not to have children. The curse cannot be broken.'

"That was the first I had heard of any curse."

"About twenty minutes after that, Lottie was born. She was so beautiful with her black hair and stunning green eyes, I knew then you would be important to me, darling."

"After Lottie was born, Sarah started haemorrhaging badly. Frank made it back to the farm and came into the room just as this tiny perfectly formed little male was born. He was so tiny, he fit into the palm of my hand. He was already gone by then, of course. We did what we could for Sarah, but it was too late. She'd lost too much blood. Frank went a little mad then. He kept going on about how Lottie had been born perfectly healthy, but her twin brother was dead. He said Lottie had stolen her

brother's life and the life of her mother. He was wrong, Lottie. I want you to know that."

"Molly, his mother, kept shouting at him that it was the curse, but he was too far gone in his grief by then."

"After the funeral he disappeared, leaving Lottie and Renee to be raised by their grandmother. The Chief sent over one of the village women who couldn't have children to help the three of you. He was still trying to make amends for the curse he had issued, but it was too late for Frank. Something broke in him that night, and he's never been the same since."

"About four years later, he returned with Ava and Marie in tow. Sometime later I found out who their mother was. I was in town one day and a woman approached me. She knew that our farm bordered the Moore's property and she was looking for Frank. She said he had missed a payment. I found out that she was a drug addict and Frank was paying

her to stay out of his life as she had been threatening to sue for custody. Not long after that conversation, I heard she had overdosed and died."

"That's the whole sad story of why Frank is the way he is. It's not an excuse for the man's behaviour, but I hope you can understand a little better now."

After the story, I was emotionally drained and sat there looking at the tears on the faces of the females around me. I saw the hurt and pain in Lottie's eyes and the anger on Renee's face.

She turned to the Chief and demanded, "Is there nothing that can be done? Are you telling me that my sisters and I might never have a live child, if all we conceive is males? Lottie is expecting now. Do you know the stress this will cause her?"

I started to speak, but the Chief stopped me with a raised hand. "I do understand, Renee, and I hate what my grandfather did. He tried to undo the curse many times, but simply wasn't able to. That is why I'm here today, as I understand your anger. Please, understand that I will continue to try and end this curse. We've all had to live with it over the years. By that I mean that it has affected my family too."

"I am going to tell you something that nobody knows. There has not been a live female born in my line since the night of the curse. So while you have no males, we have no females. It would seem that the curse rebounded on my grandfather when it was made. I make no excuse for his actions. I just wanted you to know that your family is not the only one that suffered. Because of the wicked acts of one tribe, I myself have lost three daughters to the curse."

Lottie let out a sob as she ran to the Chief and hugged him, sobbing, "I'm so sorry for you and your family."

The Chief stopped his warriors when they moved to pull her away. He held Lottie's cheeks in his hands and pressed a kiss to her forehead. "You are a good, kind, female, Lottie Moore. I thank you for your condolences. I have been blessed with my sons and you will be blessed with your daughters. Don't let this curse take any more from us than it already has. Enjoy your life and be happy. You have a strong mate and an extended family made up of fierce male and female warriors. Enjoy your offspring because they will always surprise you. Remember, if you or your sisters ever need my help, you just have to call, and some of my family or I will come."

He handed Lottie back to Kyle who had come to stand beside her.

The Chief nodded at all of us as he prepared to leave. Stopping by me, he smiled, "Annie, if you ever decide you want to be a second wife, let me know," he said, fixing me with his kind eyes.

"Thank you, Chief," I said, laughing, "But I have enough to do seeing to my own growing family. However, I will be by to share a meal with your wife this week, and I'll be sure to tell her of your kind offer." Her eyes twinkled with humour.

He let out a loud laugh at this, shaking his head. He gave me a wink, as he made to leave. "Please do, Annie. I find I quite like it when my wife is angry with me. It makes for an *'interesting'* time."

There was a pained groan from one of the younger warriors.

Still smiling, the Chief chuckled. "My son does not like to be reminded of how he came about." Soft laughter followed them as they disappeared into the darkness.

I turned to my family to see how they were doing. As expected, there were a few tears, and I could see the anxiousness on Lottie's face in regard to her pregnancy.

Jett was there reassuring Lottie and Kyle that he would scan her as soon as she was further along. I knew that we'd be able to find out the sex of my grandchild early, which was a blessing, as I didn't think any of us would be making it through the entire pregnancy without the worst kind of worry.

Sighing, I looked up at the sky. The stars twinkled in the darkness, and I wondered what made people do the things they did without considering how it might affect generations to come.

CHAPTER 24

LOTTIE

After the Chief had left, I felt drained as well as worried about what was in store for us. I'd gone from being ecstatic about my pregnancy, to frightened that it would be a boy.

The thought of losing my baby filled me with dread. I burrowed as close to Kyle as I could get, feeling his arms tighten around me.

We were all on mattresses in the rondavel. Luca and Anton had jokingly said that they wouldn't bother with chalets anymore when we all got together, since we always seemed to end up on mattresses. I, for one, needed everyone around me. Kyle was behind me and, in front of me, Renee was asleep but still holding my hand tight. Their heads butting up against us, Ava and Marie each had a hand on me or Kyle for comfort. Behind Kyle were Annie, Sean, and Rory, with Amy in between them.

The others had all found sleeping places as close to Kyle and me as possible, even Joel, who had been on edge all evening. He kept muttering about the smell of cinnamon sugar driving him nuts. None of us could figure out what he was going on about. None of the MacGregors or the Russos could smell what he was smelling.

Amy was getting concerned about her brother and how much time he was spending alone.

I decided that Kyle and I would go over later in the week and spend a night with him. One thing that tonight had shown me was that we all needed each other in order to be happy.

My heart was broken for my mother and father, and all that our family had gone through because of hate and greed.

So many lives lost for nothing, and so many more to be lost if the curse was real. I worried not only about my baby, but about future babies my sisters may have when they found their mates.

The thought of them having to go through what my grandmother and mother had gone through filled me with dread.

Lying there, I forgave my father for not having control over our situation and for losing everything due to the evil ways of men. If I ever saw him again, I'd be sure to tell him, because I didn't want hate tainting my life like it did his. I'd ensure that whatever children were born into our family would know that they were loved.

"Sleep, Angel. It'll all be alright. Didn't I tell you that you deserve only good things in life?" Kyle whispered softly against my neck where his gorilla had marked me.

Squeezing his hand that was cradling my stomach where our small bean lay, I answered, "You did, and I'll try not to worry, honey. Love you."

"Love you, Angel," I heard Kyle whisper back as I started to drift off. Before I did, I saw Renee's eyes open to look at my sleepy face. Her eyes lifted to Kyle's and then to Ava and Marie who were watching us, their eyes fierce and angry on our behalf.

CHAPTER 25

KYLE

I was the first to wake the next morning, Lottie still sleeping in my arms. There was a new tension in her face that hadn't been there before last night. I hated that this had added stress to her. Her sisters were as close to us as they could get. Ava's hand was tangled in my hair, which made me laugh considering our love-hate relationship. She thought I'd stolen her sister from her, but if she was trying to comfort me, I guess I must have worn her down some.

What would the coming weeks bring? I didn't think Lottie and I would relax until we knew the sex of our baby. Jett had told me the earliest we could find out was fourteen weeks, but we'd get a more accurate reading at eighteen weeks.

I planned on pushing to find out as early as possible so we could prepare ourselves.

Looking up, I saw Renee's eyes were open. She took hold of Ava's hand and a smile crossed her face as she looked at the grip her sister had on me.

"Do you need some help?" she queried.

"Yeah, I guess she doesn't hate me so much anymore," I said, grinning.

Renee snorted quietly. "I wouldn't bet on it. You caught her at a weak moment. That one knows how to hold a grudge, and you stole her beloved sister, remember?"

Renee managed to free me from Ava and we both got up. As it was a cool morning, I made sure to tuck the blankets around Lottie. The coffee pot had been left on the table, so I helped myself to a cup and went over to the fire pit. There I built a fire to take the chill off the morning. Renee joined me and we quietly watched the sunrise together.

After I finished my coffee, Renee stopped me from getting up by putting a hand on my arm. I looked at her in surprise.

She took a deep breath and sighed. "I wanted to thank you, Kyle, for loving Lottie the way you do, for putting her first and making sure she knows it. For too long she was an afterthought. Now that we know the history, I can understand it, but it's still hard to forgive the way he treated her. If I know her, she's probably already forgiven him, but it will take me a bit more time. I heard what you said last night that she deserves all the good things in life. If anyone does, it's Lottie, I think she's made a good start with you."

Behind me, I heard two voices in unison say, "We agree. All the good things, starting now."

Clearing my throat that suddenly felt thick with emotion, I nodded at Renee and turned to see Ava and Marie. Ava thrust a cup of coffee at me. "Here, I made you coffee like you like it. Don't get used to this treatment though," she warned, squinting at me slightly.

Taking the cup from her, I answered, "Thank you, Ava. I'll certainly try not to get used to any love you might throw at me." I couldn't help but needle her.

"Mmph," she muttered. "See that you don't."

I couldn't take her threat seriously though as she sat down next to me and laid her head on my shoulder. I laughed and dropped a kiss on her head, sipping my peace offering of coffee.

I sat like that with Lottie's sisters, enjoying the peace of the morning until we heard the rest of the group stirring behind us.

Then we went back inside to help with breakfast. The plan was to enjoy the rest of the day before packing up and going home.

Looking over at the mattresses, I saw that Lottie and Reggie were the only two still asleep. I made a plate up for Lottie and put it to the side without disturbing her. I wanted her to sleep as long as possible. I saw that Dex had done the same for Reggie.

Breakfast was a pretty quiet affair. I noticed that the Moore sisters were being given more affection than usual, a touch on the hand, a hug, or a kiss on the head. It seemed to be what they needed as they quietly accepted this show of affection.

I was pleased to see that they were slowly becoming the happy females they usually were, though a little quieter than normal. They seemed to have shaken off some of the gloom of their history during the night.

When Anton asked how they were doing, Renee shrugged and said they'd discussed it last night. They'd decided that there was nothing that could be done, so they'd just keep on living their lives. If and when any of them became pregnant, they'd deal with it then and be there to support each other no matter what happened.

Smelling Lottie's unique scent getting stronger I turned in my chair to watch her as she came closer. Her face was still soft with sleep, her eyes not yet completely open as she stumbled over to us. Getting up, I went to her and enfolded her in my arms. She shoved her face into my neck and breathed me in.

"Don't like waking up without you, honey," she muttered into my neck.

Kissing her cheek, I said, "Sorry, Angel. You needed the sleep. Tomorrow I'll wake you, I promise."

"See that you do. God, I miss coffee. I need to speak to Jett about this. It's torture," she grumbled.

Behind me, her sisters were snickering but as I liked my balls where they were,

I knew better than to poke the bear on the coffee issue.

Sitting back down, I pulled Lottie onto my lap. A hand came from behind us and wafted a small cup of coffee under her nose. She perked up immediately and grabbed at it.

"One small cup a day, Lottie. No more," Jett warned her, taking his hand from the cup.

As she took a sip of the coffee, she groaned in ecstasy, which made me instantly hard.

"Thank you, Jett. You are a saint amongst men," she stated.

Another groan came from the other side of the table. I looked up to see Dex in the same predicament as me. His mate was on his lap, sucking up her coffee like it was the last one she'd ever have.

"I agree with Lottie. The rest of you take note. Jett knows the secret to happy women," declared Reggie.

We all laughed at the two of them. Jett smirked at the rest of us, looking pleased with himself.

Looking around the table at the family my brothers and I seemed to have amassed in a short space of time, I couldn't help but be proud of the strong females that were now my sisters. I knew we'd all be okay, because this family had put up with enough heartbreak and knew how to face it and win.

After breakfast, we enjoyed the rest of the day, boating, water-skiing and, above all, laughing.

We left late in the afternoon and got home to find supper cooked and Julie waiting for us to fill her in on everything.

Next time, I would make sure she joined us, no matter what.

CHAPTER 26

LOTTIE

It had been a nerve-wracking couple of months. Everyone tried to get on with their lives, but as my belly grew so did our worries. Finally, the day came when we could find out if we were having a male or a female.

I was so anxious, my hands were sweating and I felt clammy all over. Jett drove Renee, Annie, Kyle and me into town. I was booked into the maternity of the same hospital I'd been in with my head injury.

Jett took us into the room with the ultrasound machine. He was going to do the scan so I didn't have to explain the situation to a stranger. After he dropped us off, he went off to find my notes. I lay on the bed trying not to hyperventilate.

Kyle moved to the top of the bed and cradled my face with his hands.

Smiling down at me, he said, "Seems like we've been in this position before, just changed up a bit."

Gently kissing me, he leant his forehead against mine before looking into my eyes. "All the good things, Angel, all the good things. You'll see."

"Right, are we ready?" asked Jett. I hadn't even realised that he was back in the room.

Taking a deep breath, I nodded and adjusted my clothing so Jett could do the exam. My belly had a slight round shape to it now that I was eighteen weeks. We'd decided to wait until we could be sure that I would make it past the first trimester before having a scan. So far, we'd only heard the baby's heartbeat, which Julie assured us was strong.

Jett squirted gel on me and started to move the wand around on my stomach.

Fairly quickly, we saw the outline of the baby. I was gripping Annie's hand on one side and Renee's on the other. Kyle was still standing at my head, running his fingers through my hair.

Jett was quiet as he moved the wand around. Finally, when I thought he was never going to say anything, he spoke. "There you are! Sorry, your girls were being a bit shy," he beamed at us, his face lit with happiness.

Tears ran down my face. Looking at Renee and Annie I saw they were in the same state. Lifting my eyes, I looked up at Kyle.

His eyes were filled with love as he looked down at me. "Told you, Angel. Only the good things. And look, we get two more of you. What more could I want?"

We were all a mess of emotions for the next hour or so as Jett finished up doing the important things, like measuring the babies and printing pictures by the dozen. Once that was done, Jett insisted I get seen by the midwife to make sure he hadn't missed anything.

Getting off the bed, I felt Kyle's arms surround me in a tight hug. Smiling up at him, I felt a lightness I hadn't felt since our first night by the hot springs.

Pressing my lips to his in a long, sweet kiss, I felt like my heart was going to burst with happiness. I marvelled at this male who always seemed to know what I needed. He always put me first no matter what. I knew our girls would never need to wonder if their father loved them.

I couldn't wait to let the rest of the family know so that they could all relax and we could enjoy the coming months.

EPILOGUE

LOTTIE

TWELVE YEARS LATER

THE LAKE

We were all at The Lake for Christmas as we had been every year since we started having children. This way we could all spend it together.

Anton and Luca had built a bigger rondavel just for all of us to sleep in. All these years later, everyone sleeping together in a big group continued to be the tradition.

The adults were all sitting around the fire pit watching the kids mess around in the water. I was sitting down, leaning up against a very tense Kyle, as was Dex who was sitting next to me.

We were watching our twin daughters Mia and Bella, who were in the water with Dex's twin sons Ben and James. The boys had turned thirteen but our girls were still twelve, although they would be thirteen soon. The four of them were close and did most things together, so seeing them arguing was unusual.

Neither of our girls had shifted but we were really hoping they would, so my sisters would see it and have some hope their cubs would do the same. Time was running out since they were turning thirteen soon and would be out of their twelfth year. We had all but given up on the idea that it would be them that broke the curse.

There had been a few sad losses over the years, not only for our family but also for the Chief's sons, but we had held together and supported each other. Each of my sisters had mates that were strong and put them first in all things.

None of our children knew our history. We wanted them to live their lives without the added pressure of wondering if they would shift. We'd tell them when they were older.

Our girls just assumed since their aunts, Kyle and I didn't shift, then that was why they didn't. It never seemed to bother them when they were playing with their cousins that could shift or children from the other families.

As we watched, the boys seemed to be riling the girls up about something. Dex started to get up to intervene but something made me stop him.

"Wait!" I grabbed hold of his arm. Kyle and I, Reggie and Dex stood quietly and stared, amazed.

Suddenly, where there had been two twelve-year-old girls, now there stood two small, slightly dazed gorillas.

Dex's boys were jumping up and down shouting, "You did it! You did it! We knew you could." Then they tumbled into them, taking them down onto the ground.

We all hurried toward them, shock on our faces. Getting closer, we started laughing at the two leopard cubs that were wrestling with the gorillas.

It was a surreal moment. We couldn't believe that after all this time that the curse was over.

Kyle and I ran over and grabbed our girls from the pile of children on the ground and hugged them before putting them back down to enjoy their new shapes.

I looked around at my sisters in the arms of their mates, and then at the pile of wrestling children we'd all made. All these children that had grown up together, some shifters, some not, but all having fun. The ones that were bird shifters started dive bombing the ones on the ground, making us all laugh.

As the sun went down over the water, I was held tight in the arms of my mate, who after all this time still showed me every day that he loved me.

In the distance, we heard the beating of drums coming from the direction of the Chief's village. My sisters' eyes were filled with tears. We knew that now the Chief would be able to welcome granddaughters into the world.

Annie cleared her throat, looking at all of us with raised eyebrows. "Ladies, don't you all have something to tell your mates?"

I saw the confusion on Kyle's face as I turned to him. After hearing our history, we had decided that after the girls we wouldn't have any more children. We were lucky enough with the two healthy girls we had.

But things happen and, on our anniversary at the hot springs, we had gotten a little carried away. I had been putting off telling him since I was terrified, not just because of the curse but also my age.

Lifting my eyes to his, I smiled, "I'm pregnant."

His face broke into a broad smile, filled with love. "Only the good things, Angel," he whispered, before kissing me, long and sweet.

Around us I heard shouting and laughing. Turning to look, I saw a bunch of proud looking males, although some were looking a bit shell-shocked as each of them were told they were going to be fathers again.

Happiness was a good look on our family. I couldn't believe that all the females had fallen pregnant at the same time. One thing was for sure, it was going to be an interesting year.

Later that night, we got confirmation that the beating drums we had heard was the Chief and his family welcoming two beautiful healthy granddaughters.

THE END

Acknowledgements

I would like to say a massive thank you to my fellow author and friend Cloe Rowe. Without your encouragement and help this book would never have seen the light of day. One of the best things I have ever done was contact you after reading your first book Redemption Ranch. You have been an inspiration from day one.

To the lovely Jeneveir Evans our early morning chats (well early for me, late nights for you) and suggestions have been invaluable. Thank you for taking the time from your busy schedule to help me. Keep that saga going!

My eldest daughter Helen who every day offered positive quotes and comments during this journey. I love you more than the whole world and don't know what I would do without you and your encouragement. Thank you for my beautiful book covers and making me a font just for me. Love you, baby.

To youngest, my lovely Ria, I love your snarky comments when we have to share the same space while I write. Don't ever change. Love you to the moon and back.

To my husband for always encouraging me on whatever crazy idea takes me at the time. Being there for me, always putting me first and for treating me like a queen. You are my inspiration.

To my mum who keeps our house running smoothly I honestly don't know what I would do without you. Love you.

To all my readers who took a chance on me with my first book Wild & Free and for reaching out with positive comments and suggestions. I want to say a massive

THANK YOU!

So, from the bottom of my heart thank you.

About the Author

I grew up on a cattle farm on the outskirts of a small town in Zambia, which is in Southern Central Africa. I went to school in South Africa, Zambia and finally finished my schooling in Zimbabwe. I had an amazing childhood filled with fantastic experiences. As a family, we often holidayed at Lake Kariba and I feel very privileged to have seen Victoria Falls, one of the seven wonders of the world several times.

My grandparents lived on the same farm as my parents and me. It was my grandmother, my Ouma who first introduced me to the romance genre, and I was hooked from there.

I now live happily in Jane Austen country in the UK with family.

Follow me:

Email: michelledups@yahoo.com

https://www.facebook.com/michelle.dups.5/

https://www.instagram.com/michelle_s_belle_s

www.michelledups.carrd.co

THANK YOU!

Thank you for taking the time and a chance on me, I hope you enjoy reading my books as much as I enjoy writing them. Books make life a little easier to handle in these strange times.

I write what I like to read and life is hard enough as it is, so there is little angst in my books. They all have a have a happy ending, a strong family vibe with strong alpha males and strong females.

The reason I wrote my first book Wild & Free was that the last year hasn't been the best for anyone really and I decided that I wanted to start knocking things off my bucket list. As travel was off the cards .... I decided with much encouragement from fellow authors and my family to dust off my notes from the book I started in 1999 while still living in Africa.

I hope you have enjoyed reading and finding out about Lottie and Kyle.

I love to hear from my readers so please feel free to message me on any of my social media.

If I could be so cheeky as to ask you to please leave a review, these are truly helpful to indie authors.

Much love to all my readers.

BOOKS IN THIS SERIES

Sanctuary Book 1 – WILD & FREE (Dex & Reggie)

Sanctuary Book 2 - ANGEL (Kyle & Lottie)

EXCERPTS FROM REVIEWS FOR WILD & FREE

AMAZON

COULDN'T PUT IT DOWN

The characters catch you straight away, can't wait for more in the series, was totally immersed.

GREAT NEW SHIFTER SERIES

I'm completely intrigued by this new series.

EXCERPTS FROM REVIEWS FOR WILD & FREE

GOODREADS

GREAT READ

Really enjoyed this debut book by this author. The story was great and the characters were awesome.

Printed in Great Britain
by Amazon

85758694R00171